THE MISSION HOUSE

CARYS DAVIES

GRANTA

Granta Publications, 12 Addison Avenue, London W11 4QR

First published in Great Britain by Granta Books, 2020
This paperback edition published by Granta Books, 2021

A CIP catalogue record for this book is available from the British
Library.

1 3 5 7 9 10 8 6 4 2

ISBN 978 1 78378 431 8 (paperback)
ISBN 978 1 78378 432 5 (ebook)

Typeset by Avon DataSet Ltd, 4 Arden Court, Alcester, Warwickshire

Printed and bound by CPI Group (UK) Ltd, Croydon, CR0 4YY

www.granta.com

MIX
Paper from
responsible sources
FSC® C020471

For Michael

1

As they climbed, the air cooled; by the time they were half-way up, it was chilly and fresh. 'Thank God!' said Byrd, gulping the breeze from the open window, and when the Padre asked him, what brought him here, up into the hills? Byrd said – and it felt like the truth – 'The weather.'

At Modern Stores he bought milk and Nescafé and a packet of Highfield Premium Tea, a very expensive jar of Hartley's raspberry jam, two eggs in a paper bag, and what looked and smelled like a banana muffin, which he planned to eat in the morning for his breakfast.

The Padre had told him about a short cut which would bring him up out of the hectic town to the presbytery on the hill above the church, and from the high pavement outside Modern Stores he could see the church's white spire, pointing like a compass needle into the misty sky above the messy pattern of tiled and corrugated roofs and the floaty, lightly moving tops of the trees.

'There it is,' he said aloud, because it was reassuring to be able to see exactly where he was going. Carrying his shopping and his straw hat and pulling his suitcase over the broken surface of the road, he moved towards it until he came to the broad concrete steps the Padre had described. Up he went. On his left a group of women in bright clothes hacked at the ground with small sharp tools that flashed in the weak sunlight. Then, just as the Padre had told him they would, the steps delivered him out onto a steep road above the town at a gateless opening surrounded by thick vegetation; a crooked sign on the right-hand side said: DOG IS ON DUTY.

Byrd walked in under a canopy of dripping trees along a red earth driveway puddled with water.

There was no sign of any dog, or the Padre. The bungalow was there though, in the garden next to the presbytery, as the Padre had promised, the door open invitingly.

How tired he was!

How exhausted after his weeks wandering about down on the plains: the temples and the dusty museums, the endless hotel rooms, the uncomfortable nights spent on buses and trains, the awful clamour of the auto rickshaw drivers, the intolerable heat.

At the beginning of his travels, it had all gone well enough. At his hotel next to the Danish fort in Tranquebar, a pleasant breeze had blown in off the Bay of Bengal. In the middle of the night he'd looked out of his window to see the lights of fishing boats strung out across the water, like fallen stars. In the morning, waiters had arrived at his table in crisp white jackets and scarlet headdresses and his tea had come in a silver pot. His bedroom had overflowed with sequined bolsters and gorgeous rugs, and when he'd strolled along the shore past the fishermen mending their fine white nets, they'd seemed to be sitting cross-legged in a bank of cloud.

But the hotel was more expensive than he could afford (more expensive than he thought a hotel in this country should reasonably be) and he'd moved up the coast to Pondicherry, but the Pondicherry hotels had been expensive too, and he'd been obliged to move on. For a month he'd shuttled between the cities of the interior, and everywhere he went, he found them alive with unbearable numbers of people and cars and scooters, bright lights and noise, horns and clatter and an endless beeping, the roar of engines, steam and smoke and diesel, with street vendors thronging the pavements in front of phone shops and newspaper kiosks, calling out to him about their vegetables and their fruit; he'd fought his way past men in flowing robes and men in white-collared shirts and dark trousers carrying briefcases, women in blue jeans and women in glittering saris, children in polished shoes and no shoes at all. It was overwhelming. The crippled beggars repulsed and terrified him, and he'd hurried past them with his suitcase, praying they would not reach out and catch hold of his ankle or the hem of his shorts. On top of everything, there'd been the heat.

But he was here now, and though there'd been clamour and hustle as he'd made his way through the town, it seemed to him like a gentler version of everything he'd encountered down on the plains, and best of all, he was no longer sweating.

In the cool of the evening he walked through the small, square rooms of the little bungalow: a sitting room with a fireplace and an etching of a Scottish loch and a neat, round table, in the corner a green fridge; a verandah-like room closed-in with windows, containing a desk and a huge extra-ordinary chair like a dentist's; a bedroom with a three-quarter bed, an embroidered placard on the wall above it which said, *I will be your Shield, your High Tower, the Horn of your Salvation*; a bathroom with a toilet and a sink and a big pink plastic bucket like a dustbin; a kitchen with a blue propane bottle and a two-burner stove, another sink, and shelves lined with clean newspaper. Ideal Pigeon, it said in black script on the front of the stove's white enamel.

'Well isn't this nice,' he said aloud.

He boiled the eggs and made himself a cup of tea. He unpacked his things and stowed his suitcase under the bed. He walked through all the rooms again, closing the open windows and drawing all the curtains. It was hard to imagine anything more cosy and snug.

In the kitchen he put a pan of water on to boil, then two more, until there was enough hot water in the pink bucket in his bathroom for him to stand in it and wash himself. There was still a crust of salt around his middle from the sweat which had collected there, in the heat of the morning, and dried when the train reached the cool air of the mountains. It gave him such pleasure to see it dissolve and disappear beneath his wet sponge. And then there was the novelty of putting on his pyjamas, which he hadn't worn since leaving home.

It was late when he noticed the other man's clothes, hanging limply from a forked hook on the back of the bedroom door. The door was open against the wall, and when he closed it, there they were: a red and blue plaid shirt and a pair of dark, many-pocketed trousers; a hat with ear flaps and a pom-pom.

It amazed him, what he felt when he saw them – how much he would have preferred it if they weren't there; how much, in the few short hours since he'd arrived, he'd come to think of the place as his own.

He pushed the door back against the wall so that the clothes of the absent missionary were, as they'd been before, out of sight.

On his pillow, a hot water bottle lay in a woollen cover, and he thought about boiling another pan to fill it, but he was so very tired now, and instead he climbed into the three-quarter bed and let his head sink into the cool pillow. For a little while, he read, but soon his eyes began to close, and his last thought before he slept was how lucky it was, that he and the Padre had boarded the same carriage at Mettupalayam; how lucky that they'd fallen into conversation after his joyous *Thank God!* when, half-way up, the air had cooled; what a stroke of good fortune it was, that this little bungalow was lying here in this pretty, if slightly neglected and overgrown garden, empty and available.

2

At the railway terminus the Padre had parted with Mr Hilary Byrd and they had gone their separate ways, Mr Byrd to Modern Stores to buy his supplies, the Padre to the presbytery to prepare the bungalow for his arrival.

When he had beaten the rugs and put a quilt and a hot water bottle on the bed and pegs on the wire washing line outside, when he had put fresh newspaper on the kitchen shelves and dry sticks in the grate and a bag of milk in the small green fridge in the sitting room, the Padre sat down on the stone steps outside and told the dog, Ooly, that they were expecting a visitor.

The dog's ears twitched. At the edge of the garden the leaves of the eucalyptus trees waved about in the breeze and a light rain began to fall. It fell on the Padre's head and on the dog lying in the old kitchen sink. A shallow rust-coloured lake began to form around her but she didn't seem to mind. She stayed where she was, her long throat resting on the sink's lip, her dark liquid eyes looking out across the garden, past the hydrangea bush and the banana tree and the Dorothy Perkins rose towards the cratered driveway and the gateless entrance and the road, as if this was the first piece of news that had interested her in a very long time.

3

In the days that followed, Byrd toured the town.

He visited the Botanical Gardens and the lake. He called at the King Star Chocolate Shop and bought six ounces of Fruit & Nut in a vacuum-sealed foil bag. He replenished his supplies in the market and at Modern Stores. He ate lunch at the Nazri Hotel. He walked through the jewellery district. He visited the library and Higginbotham's bookshop. At the bank opposite the Collector's Office, he changed his money, and at the CTR barber shop he had his hair trimmed and watched the cricket which was playing on a small television high up on the wall, and everywhere he went things were, as they had been down on the plains, both strange and familiar, predictable and wholly unexpected; easy to understand and indecipherable. A lot of people spoke English but a lot didn't. Some of the newspapers were in English but most weren't. Some of the buildings reminded him of home but many didn't.

In the Global Internet Cafe he composed an email to his sister, Wyn, full of details and description, and the little saga of his lucky meeting with the Padre and how it had brought him to his bungalow, and when it was finished he sent it to her, like a peace offering.

Nothing could have prepared him for the claggy, oppressive heat of the plains. He'd felt as if he were being slowly cooked, basted in the sweat with which his pale body was permanently awash, and eventually he could no longer face doing battle with it. For a whole week he didn't go outside; he stayed in his hotel room with the ceiling fan going and the air conditioning on, and then one evening he'd gone down to the bar and heard a group of German tourists talking about a slow blue train with decorated glass windows that would bring him up out of the roasting cauldron of the plains into the cool air of the mountains. In the morning he'd packed his suitcase and taken a taxi to Mettupalayam and by 7 o'clock he'd been in his seat, high up on the winding track, looking down upon a brown river sliding between big boulders and small, broken rocks.

He liked his bungalow more and more.

He'd been shopping again, at Modern Stores and in the market, and all his jars and packets were arranged on the newspaper-covered shelves in his kitchen; his fruit and his vegetables stowed away on the tiered orange plastic stand next to the Ideal Pigeon stove; his books in a pile on his desk, his pyjamas under his pillow. Through the windows of the verandah-like room at the front, he could see out across the valley to the other side, beyond the town, to the mist-shrouded forests and bright, tea-covered slopes.

He also liked the presbytery garden – its combination of the exotic and the familiar: the rhubarb and the multi-coloured asters, the penstemons and the snapdragons, the elderflower and the sweet williams, all mixed in with the banana tree and the eucalyptus and some kind of huge, almost plastic-looking green shrub with giant red flowers which Wyn might have known the name of but which he couldn't identify.

The only irritating thing was the black dog. He hadn't noticed it the day he arrived, but it lay, almost all the time, in a white sink on the ground next to the boiler house behind the presbytery. The only time he'd seen it move was when it climbed out of the sink and followed him to the door of his bungalow, as if it expected to be allowed inside.

The Padre himself came and went quietly and unobtrusively. Byrd saw him most mornings, setting off on an ancient motorbike with a spare tyre on the back, inside a beige vinyl cover that said *Padre Andrew*.

He and his brothers had all been named for the apostles, said the Padre cheerfully when he saw Hilary Byrd looking at the tyre. They'd been baptised at the Immanuel Church in Coimbatore – their father had worked at the post office there. 'My older brother is Thaddeus. The others are James and Philip. Thaddeus is dead now. The other two are in Chennai. I am the only one of us who went into the church.'

He was short and round and very dark, bald and old, and most of the time he was dressed as he'd been on the day of their first meeting, in a too-large fleece hat and a green jacket; long trousers and a scarf wound around his neck like a snowman's. He looked a little, thought Byrd, like Paddington Bear.

'Settling in, Mr Byrd, sir?' he said at the end of a few days from the seat of his motorbike at the presbytery's gateless opening when he was coming in and Byrd was going out, and Byrd said, 'Yes!' He liked his bungalow very much, he liked the town. There was a lot he didn't understand but even so, he was feeling very much at home.

The Padre tilted his head to one side. He looked pleased – no, he looked more than pleased. He looked delighted, as if nothing in the world could make him happier than Mr Hilary Byrd settling in and liking the town and feeling very much at home. Perhaps, he said, Mr Byrd would have dinner with him one evening, in the presbytery? Tomorrow, perhaps? If he would like that?

Byrd said he would like that very much.

The Padre beamed and clapped his hands. He seemed ready to explode with delight.

'Good. I will tell Priscilla.'

And then he was moving off, bouncing away along the puddled red driveway towards the front door of the presbytery.

Byrd watched him kick out the stand on his motorbike and disappear into the house.

Priscilla?

He had not known there was anyone else here. He had thought he was alone with the Padre and the dog.

4

At the terminus, the day Byrd arrived, the auto rickshaw drivers had called out to him, *Sir! Sir!* They had folded back the dripping blue tarpaulins of their tiny black and yellow vehicles and gestured for him to enter their damp and ramshackle interiors.

One of them – a short, old, desperate-looking man in tracksuit bottoms and a flapping shirt – had moved towards him, advancing at a steady forward-tilting trundle and already speaking to him. *Sir!* Byrd had taken a step back. His hand moved lightly, instinctively, to the nylon money belt around his middle. He hated the way these people made him feel both guilty and afraid. He wished he'd gone with the Padre – wished he had not said that he would do his shopping first, and then make his own way up to the presbytery by himself. He'd raised his chin and fastened his gaze on the white spire of the church in the middle distance which the Padre had promised would lead him in the right direction. Even so, he could still feel, and smell, the old man – close to him now, just a little to his left. *Please, sir.* Dark creased hands with stubby prayer-laced fingers, separated to fan a wallet of cracked and faded photographs, had appeared at the edge of Byrd's vision. Glancing down he saw a pair of dirty feet, one wearing a black flip-flop and the other a red plastic clog. Close to Byrd's face, a lilting obsequious voice spoke. 'Botanical Gardens, sir.

Lake. Tea Plantation. Savoy Hotel. King Star Chocolate Shop. Racecourse. 500 rupees. Whole day. Please, sir.'

If Wyn had been with him she would have gone striding off into the throng by now, plied her way through the press of bodies saying, *Excuse me, excuse me*, and found someone reliable to take them shopping and on up to the presbytery. She would have come back smiling and certain and taken him by the arm and said, 'This way, Hilary, this way.' She would have fought off anyone who had the impression that Hilary Byrd was adrift, somehow, here in the hills; that his long-wristed hand was there for the taking, to be led away through the teeming streets or off into the tree-choked forests of wattle and eucalyptus. But Wyn was not with him, and Byrd had been quite alone and very anxious about being drawn into anything unwanted; about being taken to some place he didn't want to go. It had happened to him everywhere, time and again: in Chennai and Trichy and Thanjavur, when he was making his aimless and uncomfortable way across the roasting plains, he'd found himself enticed into taxis and auto rickshaws by their eager and insistent drivers – taken to countless shops and temples and palaces he didn't want to visit and then asked for more money than he wanted to pay.

Do not make eye contact with the drivers of auto rickshaws, said his guidebook. *Once you make eye contact, you are lost*. It was true. Over and over, down on the plains, he had repeated the same mistake.

'Please, sir,' said the voice. 'I am begging you. Please.'

5

For dinner there was a large ugly-headed fish, sambar, dosas, and a dish of fryums, which seemed to be the Padre's favourite food – he munched almost exclusively on the multi-coloured snacks while Byrd tried to concentrate on his fish and his rice.

There was a brief moment of awkwardness when they began – Byrd plunging into his plate without hesitation as soon as he was served, the Padre joining his hands together in prayer to say a short grace.

'Forgive me –' Byrd managed through a large mouthful of fish, but the Padre only smiled and waved his hand as if to say it didn't matter, though he did tilt his head to one side and ask – in the same gently curious way he'd asked Byrd on the train what brought him up into the hills – 'You are a Christian, sir?'

Byrd, his mouth full, shook his head, swallowed. 'No, Lord, no – I mean, no. Sorry. No.'

He was blushing, he could feel the blood rush into the roots of his thin hair. It had not occurred to him that he was supposed to be a Christian; that the Padre, perhaps, had assumed it; that it might be a condition of him renting the missionary's cosy bungalow.

He began to burble. 'I mean, you know, I was brought up going to church but as to any belief, no. None at all, I'm afraid. I'm sorry if –' but the Padre interrupted him. He told Hilary

Byrd not to be sorry, it wasn't important, he had only been curious, he hadn't meant to pry.

All through the rest of the dinner, Priscilla came and went. She brought more water and a re-fill of fryums for the Padre. She cleared their dishes and disappeared and returned with a plate of sweet limes, quartered and sprinkled with salt. She fetched and she carried, and every so often, while Byrd and the Padre ate and talked, Byrd found himself looking at her.

She was small, about five feet tall, and appeared to be about twenty years old, perhaps a little older, it was hard to say. The skin of her face was very dark, darker even than the Padre's, and she had a leather boot at the end of her right leg. When Byrd glanced at her she looked down at her hands and he saw that she had no thumbs.

6

In the evenings, in his hut by the river, the old man, Jamshed, wrote down in English, in a graph-paper exercise book from Higginbotham's bookshop, the significant events of his days. He was proud of his English and practised it whenever he could.

Tonight, on a fresh page and from time to time consulting the battered brick-sized Collins dictionary given to him by his old friend, Prem, he described how he'd gone as usual to the terminus of the mountain railway and waited for the slow blue train. How he'd watched the new tourists and the new do-gooding people come out of the ticket hall into the street. How the younger drivers had darted forwards as they always did until there were hardly any tourists and do-gooding people left.

One fat lady, (he wrote) *size of house.*

One family with red bags. One mother, one father, one girl, one boy.

Two big hippies maybe the same age as Ravi only not with Ravi's moustache and big hairstyle. Ponytails only, beards.

Fat lady, family, big hippies, all saying NO!

They had all gone hurrying past and climbed into the autos of the other drivers, and then the cold unfriendly man had appeared.

Skinny and tall like a eucalyptus tree, his straw hat hanging from his hand like a big useless leaf. Maybe a tourist, maybe a do-gooding person, it was hard to say.

The man had stood without moving. Still as a pole, he'd looked down his giant nose at the jostling drivers and the line of yellow autos out in the street.

'Sir! Sir!' Jamshed had called out, wishing the other drivers were not also shouting, 'Sir! Sir!' He'd scurried closer, hating the noisy racket of his ancient flip-flop and his ugly broken clog. He was hungry and he was thinking of the stupid promise he'd made to his crazy nephew, Ravi.

He could see the fat bulge of a money belt around the tall man's waist at the top of his long, tea-coloured shorts. 'Sir!' he'd called out again, pulling out the wallet of photographs from the breast pocket of his WORLD CLASS shirt, wishing the pictures weren't so cloudy and dull, wishing the wallet's plastic didn't stick to them like that, and make the town sights look like they were sinking underwater – the Botanical Gardens and the Assembly Rooms and the Savoy Hotel, the racecourse and the chocolate shop and the Highfield tea plantation. He'd spat on the wallet and polished it with the corner of his worn-out shirt, calling out over the other drivers, 'Sir! Sir! Please! This way! Come! 500 rupees only, whole day! Please, sir!'

But the cold unfriendly foreigner had stuck his giant nose in the air and his pointy elbow in Jamshed's chest. He'd dragged his suitcase wheel over Jamshed's unprotected foot and gone striding across the road, into the ocean of people on the other side, and vanished.

The old driver paused with his ballpoint pen above the graph-paper page, unsure what else to write. He put the point of the pen back inside its blue plastic lid; hesitated. Pictured the fat money belt and the man's long, anxious face, his useless hat and heavy suitcase. He took the lid off the pen again and held it above the paper, wanting to write more about the tall unfriendly foreigner but not knowing quite what it was he wanted to say.

That night he slept fitfully. In the morning, at the river, he washed his trousers and his shirt, and on the warm corrugated roof of his hut, before the rain returned, spread them out in the sun. He gave his black flip-flop and his red clog a wipe, and opened his journal, a picture in his mind again of the tall man's long, anxious face and his fat money belt. He still wasn't sure what it was he should have written before he closed his journal before going to bed, though on balance, he thought it was probably: *Tomorrow: Look for cold unfriendly man.*

Pictures of the tall foreigner had drifted all night through his interrupted sleep and short, broken dreams – sharp, detailed images in which he saw the man again and again: not only his suitcase and his money belt, his thick-soled sandals and straw hat, but also his pale blinking eyes and long anxious face; the way he'd looked out at the town with a kind of bewildered hope.

All night while Jamshed had lain in his bed – when he

closed his eyes and when he'd opened them – the man had been there in the dark.

The whole thing filled him with uncertainty.

He shook out the blanket on his bed and folded it into quarters. He straightened his journal and his dictionary and checked the gas was off. He gave his clog another wipe and picked up his keys.

Then he stepped out into the street, locked the J. J. Legge padlock that secured the wooden door to the rest of his tin hut, and set off.

7

'She likes you,' said the Padre.

Byrd hadn't seen him standing there.

Dressed in his fleece hat and his snowman's scarf, he seemed to have emerged from behind the hydrangea bush. He held a pair of rusty secateurs. Damp grass clung to the mottled blades. Byrd had no idea what to say – he thought of the room where they'd dined, dim in the foggy twilight, the drizzle of the day outside beyond the long windows, the different dishes spread out between the two of them, Priscilla coming and going quietly on her clumping boot, the Padre munching happily on the fryums and chatting about the choir and last week's concert by the girls from St Cecilia's school; about the problem of the fallen gravestones in the churchyard; about his difficulties with Miss Moreland, the Australian organist who insisted on playing a steady two beats behind the singing congregation.

She likes you.

Byrd experienced a rush of horror, not unlike but at the same time more intense than the feeling he had when he was being pursued by the auto rickshaw drivers: a feeling of fear mixed with guilt. The Padre was smiling happily at him, and Byrd had the impression – fleetingly to be sure but no less appallingly for that – that somehow, crazily and without being aware of it, he had made some sort of overture with regard to the unfortunate girl, Priscilla, and the Padre was now going to talk to him about it.

Then the Padre gestured at the dog in her sink and Byrd realised his mistake.

Ooly sat with her nose on the lip of the sink. She was looking at Hilary Byrd with what seemed like frank, intense longing.

'Be careful, Mr Byrd,' said the Padre, chuckling. 'She is a very bad dog.'

8

The old driver, Jamshed, had been looking now, for five days. He'd spent each one moving between all the likely places, waiting in his auto and scanning the crowds. He'd stopped at all the different entrances to the market and outside the Botanical Gardens, at Modern Stores and the Global Internet Cafe and the old racecourse, at the Nazri Hotel and the Savoy. He'd gone to the lake, and back once more to the train terminus in case the man had gone down to Coonoor for the day to visit the barracks or the arboretum or the tea plantation. Cruising the streets, looking left and right in search of the tall foreigner, cutting the engine on the hills to save fuel, cursing every bus and horse and tartan-skirted schoolgirl that blocked his path or his vision, Jamshed circled the town. Once, for a moment, he thought he glimpsed the straw crown of the man's hat exiting the internet cafe, but it wasn't him, it was only his nephew, Ravi, wearing his white Stetson.

'Ravi! Hey, boy!' he called out.

He always spoke to Ravi in English. He spoke to practically everyone he could in English. English was his only advantage over the younger drivers with the tourists and the do-gooding people. His English was far better than the younger drivers'. Some of them hardly spoke a word. Ravi's English was good. Ravi was sharp, had picked it up from the television. Ravi had an American accent.

But Ravi hadn't seen the tall foreigner. Ravi wanted to know when his uncle would have the money. Ravi said he had to go now. Ravi said he had to see a man about a horse.

Jamshed watched his nephew go.

A horse?

The old man shook his head. Everything Ravi said made him anxious these days. He felt caught between wanting to encourage the boy's crazy plan, and standing in its way.

What a sight the boy was in his American hat! Jamshed watched as a small barefoot girl in a dirty sari and a brown V-neck jumper ran in front of his nephew and held out her hand. All along the pavement men squatted in front of tiny stoves, soldering rings and necklaces. An old woman shelled peanuts and a young one laid out yellow gourds on a black cloth. Above the housewares store was the big green sign that said PERMANENT LIFE CURE GUARANTEED, and past it all, along the crowded street, the big white Stetson moved rapidly off, growing smaller and smaller until eventually Jamshed couldn't see it any more. 'Ah, Ravi,' he muttered softly, and slowly eased his old auto back into the traffic to resume his search for the man.

9

'Take some flowers and put them in Mr Byrd's bungalow. A new cloth also, for his table.'

'Yes, Uncle.'

From the front door of the presbytery, beneath the pan-tiled porch, Priscilla waved goodbye to the Padre, who was going to talk to the stone mason about the falling headstones in the churchyard. She had not been inside the mission house since Mr Byrd came; she'd been in town the morning he arrived, and the Padre had cleaned and prepared the place himself. Inside the presbytery she made her clumping uneven way up the wide creaking stairs and along the long worn-out rug on the landing to the small room at the back of the house which had once belonged to the Padre's daughter, to fetch the new cloth for Mr Hilary Byrd's table.

Opposite the linen cupboard, on the floor, was the metal chest, which she tried not to look at. It was an ordinary blue one, like the ones for sale at the market. Indeed, she was fairly sure the Padre had bought it there. She paused, still trying not to look at it, then took the key from its hiding place inside the china sheep and knelt down. She lifted the lid and took stock of its contents once again. Nothing had been added since she last looked. Kneeling on her leather boot, her mouth slightly open, her top teeth resting lightly in the shallow furrow they had made over the years in her bottom lip, she gazed for a moment or two into the trunk, then gently closed the lid, crossed the room to the linen cupboard, picked a cloth from the top of the pile, and clumped back down the creaking stairs into the hall and along the passage to the kitchen and out into the little yard behind the house where the boiler house and Ooly's sink were and, beyond them, the small peppermint-green mission house which was usually occupied by the Canadian missionary, Mr Henry Page, but was for the time being rented by Mr Hilary Byrd from Petts Wood UK.

When she knocked, he came to the door and she saw that he'd been eating his breakfast. There was a bowl and a cup on the table and he stood before her with a napkin tucked by one corner into the top of his pyjamas. He thanked her for the new cloth and said the flowers were very nice.

He was about the same height as Mr Page, but quieter, and much older.

Later, she stood with the Padre at the presbytery window, watching Mr Hilary Byrd walking in along the red puddled driveway. He was eating something from a small shiny bag.

'He has discovered the chocolate shop,' observed the Padre.

'Yes, Uncle.'

'He seems like a good man.'

'Yes, Uncle.'

Then Byrd, with his guidebook in one hand and the open silver envelope of Fruit & Nut in the other, turned onto the path that led across the garden from the driveway to his bungalow. He walked past the hydrangea, the banana tree, the Dorothy Perkins rose.

As he passed the boiler house, the dog, Ooly, climbed out of her sink and fell into step behind him. At the bungalow door, when he stopped to fish his key from his pocket, she sat looking up at him, as if she believed he might allow her inside, but he didn't, he closed the door in her face, and after sitting there for a little while, looking up at the closed door, she turned mournfully away and went back down the steps and climbed into her sink.

'Poor Ooly!' said the Padre. 'I think she is falling in love with our Mr Byrd!'

10

Byrd remembered the beginning of his fall, and the end of it, but not the middle, though he thought he must have gone shooting down the steps on his back, like someone competing in the luge.

He remembered being lost in the market. He remembered looking for something he recognised, some landmark that would indicate the right direction, a way out. He remembered blundering through a maze of passageways hung with meat and cloth and shoes and handbags and thousands and thousands of bananas and lined with people calling out to him, wanting him to buy things. He remembered slipping on the slushy pile of vegetable peelings. He remembered the cold crack of his face on the street, and that when he opened his eyes he was looking at a row of dirty toes, a black flip-flop, a red plastic clog, and into the oily blood-shot whites of a pair of eyes. *Do not make eye contact,* he remembered thinking. *Once you make eye contact, you are lost.* He remembered a bag of ice-cold milk pressed against his cheek, a voice.

'For swelling, sir.'

Outside now, it was light: a pale watery gleam shone between the heavy curtains above his head where they did not quite meet. The hot water bottle in its woollen cover beneath his feet was warm. He had no idea how long he'd slept. He touched his cheek. It felt puffy and tender and sore. He reached up and drew back one of the curtains and wiped the moisture from the glass with the sleeve of his sweater until there was a clear circle like a porthole. Streamers of white cloud drifted in a grey sky, like frills of foam on the ocean. On the linoleum floor next to his bed the tartan blanket from the verandah room had been neatly folded as if someone had recently slept beneath it, on the floor. He smelled warm milk, woodsmoke.

His face in the mirror was a dark quilt of navy and black, his left eye swollen and red and closed, like a pair of lips. His left buttock hurt when he moved, his hip was very sore, his head woozy.

In his sitting room the fire burned hot and fragrant and there was an old man stooping over it wearing a greyish short-sleeved shirt that had seen better days. In a black machine-stitched semi-circle across the back of it, Byrd saw the words WORLD CLASS, and like the bag of milk and the dirty toes, he remembered them. They had floated in front of his eyes on the cold, uncomfortable journey to the presbytery, and he thought he may even have held onto them on his way up the concrete steps to his bungalow; he remembered the different textures of the stitching and the thin cloth beneath his hand.

As near to the heat as it could go, the old man had dragged the enormous chair that had so intrigued Byrd when he first arrived, and which he'd since discovered, by way of a small brass plaque on the chair's right arm, was called a Carter's Nest For Rest. The old man had extended every possible appendage – the padded neck-rest, the footplate, the pipe-rack, the book stand, the small Bakelite tray, on which, now, he placed a cup of hot sweet tea.

Jamshed did not believe in miracles, but it did seem to

him like a kind of miracle that the Englishman's accident had taken place just as he was driving past the foot of the market steps, looking for him. He bowed his head and motioned to Byrd to sit.

His name was Jamshed, he said.

'Thank you, Jamshed,' said Byrd. 'You're very kind.'

In the days and weeks that followed, the old man ferried Hilary Byrd all over town.

He drove him to the Botanical Gardens and the market, to the jewellery district and the bank, to Modern Stores and Higginbotham's bookshop and the post office; to the Global Internet Cafe and the Assembly Rooms and the King Star Chocolate Shop; to the library and the lake.

It terrified Byrd, the way they sped along in the middle of the road into the path of the oncoming traffic; the way the old man brought them within inches of crowded buses and gigantic fruit trucks, announcing their presence with nothing more than the squeezing of a green rubber horn that made a sound like a mechanical mouse Byrd had owned as a child.

Today, on the hill from the presbytery into the town, the old man swerved almost the whole way across the road to bypass a pile of rocks and eucalyptus branches.

'Jesus Christ, Jamshed, what was that?'

'Warning, sir. Repairing pothole.'

Byrd's heart raced. He shook his head and blew out his cheeks, which still hurt a little from his fall.

'You live in a dangerous country, Jamshed.'

For the next ten minutes, as they puttered along past the

police station and the bank and the Collector's Office, Byrd
made a list of the dangers he'd had to contend with since he
left home: his encounter in Chennai with a metal post that
had sliced open his shin and filled his shoe with blood; his
diarrhoea in Thanjavur; his headlong fall, here, down the
lumpy steps outside the market. Only last night, when he was
heading out for a walk, the Padre had thrust a torch into his
hand. 'Take this, Mr Byrd. Otherwise you might fall into a
drain and drown.'

At the same moment, the old man swerved to avoid another
warning pile of rocks and foliage.

'Every time I get into this vehicle, Jamshed, I feel as if I'm
taking my life in my hands. I'd be safer if I were a cow or a goat
or that mangy horse we just passed back there.'

The old man's eyes flicked to the tiny mirror suspended
from the ceiling in front of the windshield. Byrd's face was
still an ugly patchwork of black and blue, bleeding now into
brown and yellow.

The old man looked sorrowful. 'Sir doesn't like it here.'

'Sir does like it here. I'm just saying it's not the safest place
for a tourist to come.'

'I will look after you, sir.'

'Thank you, Jamshed. That's very reassuring.'

For the remainder of their short journey they rode in
silence. Byrd was rocked to and fro by the movement of the
speeding auto. At the market he climbed out and the old
man waited. Byrd bought bananas and lychees and a bag of
pistachio nuts for himself and a box of Arabian dates to send
to Wyn. After that they headed up the hill, in the direction
of the lake. At times the tiny vehicle's straining progress was

almost painful, as if the two of them were riding a dying mule, but at the top of the hill Jamshed cut the engine and they began their swift cruising descent on the other side and Byrd loved this – in spite of all his fear of travelling at speed in the old man's flimsy auto, it was thrilling. He had never skied but he thought skiing must be like this. The cool breeze rushing past his cheek. The glitter of silver-green trees.

11

In due course, the old driver, Jamshed, will be questioned about the tall tourist, Mr Hilary Byrd.

In a leaf-green room with a small high window and a broken electric heater he will sit for hours during the investigation on a moulded plastic chair and tell the brown-uniformed policeman that looking at the tall Englishman that first day at the terminus, he had seen only money.

Money so that the tank of his auto could always be full, so he did not have to beg his customers for a 100 rupee note when they'd barely set off so he could call at the Bharat Petroleum Station to buy fuel for his empty tank. Money for a pair of shoes which matched. Money for his nephew's crazy costume.

'Don't leave anything out,' the policeman will say and the old man will nod. Even though there are certain details, now, that do not seem important.

Please, sir, he had begged the tall Englishman but the tall Englishman wouldn't even look at him. He had stood straight as a pole with his big bony nose in the air looking out towards the market and the town as if he'd heard nothing, as if he could not even see him or hear him. Jamshed had riffled the photographs beneath his thumb in their greasy plastic wallet, all the chief tourist attractions of the town – the Botanical Gardens, the Assembly Rooms, the Savoy Hotel, the chocolate shop, the lake, the racecourse – but the tall man had shooed him away like a fly and walked away from the railway terminus with long, hurrying strides, pulling his big suitcase behind him on its smooth-rolling wheels.

For a week (the old driver will tell the brown-uniformed policeman) he'd circled the town, hoping to see the tall man and entice him into his auto. One day's excursion, five hundred rupees. That's what he'd hoped for. To drive him around all day and any other day as well, whenever he needed an auto.

The policeman will clasp his hands together. He will lean forward across the small metal table separating him from the old driver and say, 'Yes, but why Mr Hilary Byrd? Why him?' The town was full of tourists and charity workers and all of them had money. What was it that had made the old driver pursue the Englishman all over town for five days until he found him?

In a quiet, almost inaudible voice Jamshed will say he doesn't know, because even though he will be afraid of this policeman, he will also be determined that there are some things he will not tell him.

The policeman will lean back in his chair and rock himself gently on the rear two legs. The old auto driver will have stopped speaking and will be looking off to the side, as if he is replaying some scene, or series of scenes, in his head. The policeman will wonder what he's hiding. He's been surprised many times in the course of his career, to discover what sort of improbable things people are capable of, and if there's anything he knows for certain, it's that people are endlessly mysterious and unpredictable. They tell the truth and they lie; they are direct and they are devious, they are rational and they are irrational. He is not yet sure which category this old man falls into, though he strikes him as the shifty, secretive type.

'*Why me, Jamshed?*'

What would the old driver have said if Hilary Byrd himself, at the beginning of it all, had ever asked?

Would Jamshed have said – more or less as he will eventually say to the policeman – that it was because Mr Hilary Byrd, in spite of his haughty nose stuck high in the air, seemed to have no clue about where he was going or how to get there, and that he was likely, therefore, to be an especially profitable sort of tourist – one who, if he would just step into Jamshed's cab, would do so again and again?

Or would he have shrugged, and said, 'Maybe useless hat. Maybe long sad face.' Would he have said that he didn't know and he couldn't explain it – that in the beginning, things had been one way, and eventually, they'd been another.

The brown-uniformed policeman will stretch and yawn, because this has been going on for a while now. He will tap the point of his ballpoint pen on his notepad and ask Jamshed again, what it was that had made him follow the Englishman like that, day after day, all over town?

But Jamshed will say that all he knows for certain is what he has already said: that he'd looked at the big Englishman that day and seen only money – only the promise, the chance, of a steady week's work. Money for a new pair of shoes and a cup of tea at the market. Money for his nephew.

The policeman will look sceptical, but he will nod, and ask, what was this nephew's name?

'Ravi,' the old driver will say.

'And where is Ravi now?'

'Gone, sir.'

12

The Botanical Gardens, Byrd wrote, *were laid out in 1848 by a Scotsman called William McIvor, from Kew.*

He paused, thinking of his letter falling onto the mat at home, Wyn opening it. She seemed impossibly far away.

To begin with, he continued, *the idea was just to provide a place where the British settlers could grow vegetables. Where once there'd been a forest and a swamp, there was soon a sort of giant allotment where (for an annual subscription of 3 rupees) they could come and dig up what they wanted. Cabbages, I suppose, and potatoes, peas and leeks and carrots and Brussels sprouts and whatever else they were used to eating which they thought would do well in this humid and temperate climate.*

Once McIvor got stuck in though, it all turned into something a lot grander. He began importing plants for the purposes of medical and scientific research. But the overwhelming impression you have, walking along the winding tree-lined paths and around the lawns and ponds and past the rose gardens and the herbaceous borders and the bandstand, is how at home a garden like this must have made the settlers feel.

I was in there for two hours today. Strolling around and poking my nose into the greenhouses, looking at the ferns. When I came out, the old man I told you about, the one who rescued me, was sitting at the kerb in his little cab, waiting.

You'll find it hard to believe, but I've got into the habit of sitting on the floor of his cab, leaning on the rail just behind his seat, talking. It's true. I find it surprisingly relaxing. Much better than being in that horrible room with Kerrigan. The old man says very little, but I think he can just about hear me over the traffic because from time to time he contributes a well-chosen word or two. Today when I'd finished in the Gardens and we were driving around, I started telling him about their history — the whole business of the vegetable allotment and all the peas and carrots and Brussels sprouts, and then the formal laying out, and McIvor shipping in all kinds of non-native species — all his cedars and cypresses, his junipers and oaks, his lupins and ferns and pansies and begonias. If the old man knew about it all already, he didn't say so, he just carried on driving me through the teeming streets — which, by the way, he does for a very reasonable price and also, I've come to think, not recklessly, as I'd thought at first, but with great care. Even though my cheek's hardly sore now and sudden jolts don't cause me any particular pain (the puffy black and blue has faded over the past few days to a rather sickly green and yellow), he still transports me with what seems like a kind of anxious circumspection — whizzing and weaving around cars and bicycles and scooters, people, trucks, buses, animals and all the other racing autos. It's a strange feeling, because the whole thing is undoubtedly dangerous, but I feel like something precious being carried in a box. A jewel, or an egg.

Anyway, after the Botanical Gardens I asked him to wait while I went to the Assembly Rooms. I went into Modern Stores first to buy a bag of Nutties (which turned out to be a bit like Maltesers) and then, in the Assembly Rooms, I sat in a box on the upper floor and watched Raiders of the Lost Ark *in Hindi, or maybe Tamil, I'm not sure which. When I came out, back into the day, the rain*

*had stopped and the old man was there waiting for me at the
kerbside and I felt more relaxed and happy than I have for a very
long time.*

*Back in the rear of the cab I told him what a good day it had
been, and how well I felt; how comfortable and at home.*

*'Yes, sir,' he said, letting in the handbrake and drifting gently
into the swiftly moving traffic. 'Like lupin, sir. Or Brussel sprout.'*

13

Up in the presbytery the Padre was writing his sermon and eating fryums and talking to his dead wife.

His wife would know what to do if she was here. She would know how to make all the proper plans and arrange everything and bring the whole thing off.

'But don't worry, Vallie-girl,' he said, addressing his departed wife in the large, shabby and once lovely drawing room where for four and a half decades she had sat by the fire, reading and doing her embroidery while he wrote at his desk. 'I am not dead yet. I will work it out somehow.'

A year ago, there'd been a possibility.

A year ago, he'd gone to the market on his two-wheeler and brought back a metal chest on the back of it and begun to put a few things inside, and for a while everything had seemed promising but nothing, in the end, had come of his early conversations with the family.

Well. They would have to see how they got on.

He laid down his pen. He was tired. More and more, there were times when he thought he would like to go to the bishop and say he was finished, now, with his work – that he had given his life to it and now he would rest, and yet his work did not *feel* finished. Not just because of Priscilla, but because of everything else – his feeling that he must stay put and not let himself be browbeaten, or worse.

It was true this was not Gujarat or Uttar Pradesh or Orissa. No one here had demolished a mosque because they wanted a temple in its place. No one had ransacked all the town's churches and sent the congregation fleeing into the forest. There'd been no Muslim dead, no Christian priests lynched, no nuns raped, no young boys burned in their father's car. There'd been no riots, no men with sticks and iron rods and sun-coloured flags beating drums. As far as he knew there were no camps full of young men in brown shorts and white shirts and little black hats.

But still, he worried. It was like a storm which kept rising and then abating, and he wondered if his daughter was right, that it was gathering its strength and when it came again, it would be stronger and more organised and more determined than before.

A week ago he'd woken sweating from a dream in which he'd been beaten and paraded naked through the streets on a donkey.

'Ah, Vallie. What to do?'

He stood up and went to the window and looked out across the garden to where Priscilla was sweeping fallen eucalyptus leaves from the driveway, and through the open door, he called to her. 'Come, Priscilla! The beggars will be here!' and together Priscilla and the Padre fetched the big buckets from the kitchen store and went out to the presbytery's gateless entrance where the beggars were already gathering, and for an hour or so they distributed rice and dal.

The Padre also straightened the crooked sign at the entrance that said DOG IS ON DUTY and tore away the vegetation which had grown in front of it – not that he believed the sign would really deter anyone who wanted to come in. If someone decided one day that it was what they were going to do, then they would do it, and there was nothing he would be able to do to stop them, except pray to the Lord Jesus.

It was his daughter and her American husband in California who had insisted on the sign. She'd always fussed about his health – about his diet and whether he was taking any exercise, was always reminding him that he was seventy-five not twenty-five – but these days, especially after the trouble in Kandhamal, she worried about all of this too. 'Please, Daddy,' she'd said on the phone. 'At least put a sign up or something.' So he had. A blue and white plastic one from Modern Stores. He looked at it now and couldn't help chuckling, just a little. The idea of Ooly ever being on duty! The idea of Ooly doing anything other than lying in her sink, looking depressed beyond words!

He hadn't told his daughter about last year's fire in the church. He'd said nothing, in fact, to anyone about it. Not to Miss Moreland, the Australian organist, nor to Mr Henry Page, the Canadian missionary, nor to Priscilla, nor to anyone in the congregation. It would only have frightened people, and that, after all, was what was wanted. There'd been no serious damage, only a stack of hymnals and prayer books burned, just inside the door; a pile of cooling white ash and charred leather when he arrived there very early on a Saturday morning to change the flowers in the chancel. He'd swept up the remnants of the books and dug a hole at the perimeter of the churchyard and buried them, thinking as he did so that if Miss Moreland or Mr Page or Priscilla or anyone else asked why there weren't so many hymnals and prayer books as before, he would say he'd given them away to another church. But no one, as it turned out, had asked. They'd had so many books in the first place, and the fire had not been a big one.

'Here, Priscilla,' he said. 'Help me with these old buckets,' and together they gathered the big containers which had been full of rice and dal and were now empty and began the walk back along the drive to the presbytery.

'The Lord be with you,' he called softly over his shoulder to the beggars as they made their way down the wide concrete steps, back into the town.

14

'Please, Uncle.'

'No, boy!'

Ravi stood before the old man in full costume: red-piped white shirt, blue jeans, fringed real leather waistcoat. Piebald imitation-suede chaps, also with fringes. Bootlace tie. Black, silver-toed cowboy boots. White Stetson.

Jamshed surveyed the elaborate outfit hanging off his nephew's stick-thin frame, some parts tight and some parts loose; the waves of glossy black hair extravagantly styled across his forehead beneath the brim of the giant hat; his big moustache.

He'd been a sight before, just with the hat, but this!

Ravi said he was very grateful for the costume. All he needed now was the horse. The horse would be part of his look, his whole act.

'Stupid boy,' said Jamshed, exasperated and more worried than ever by the scope and strangeness of his nephew's dreams. He shook his old head and pointed to the boy's CDs. 'Show me which one has a horse.'

Ravi said none of them did. The horse was his idea, it would make him stand out.

Jamshed shuffled through the rest of the discs, turning them over and looking at them, back and front. Johnny Cash, Lyle Lovett. Randy Travis. Garth Brooks.

He tapped them all with a stubby finger. 'See. No horses.'

In two weeks he'd earned more money driving Mr Hilary Byrd from Petts Wood UK than he usually made in two months. 'Here, boy,' he'd said to his nephew at the end of the first week. 'For cowboy boots and piebald chaps and fringed waistcoat,' ticking off in his mind some of the items the boy had told him he needed. Ravi had thrown his arms around him, kissed his two old cheeks.

After another week there'd been enough for the piped shirt and a second-hand guitar. Ravi had kissed his uncle then too.

Now Ravi snatched up his guitar and pulled open the wooden door in the tin wall of Jamshed's shack. Said he was going out. Said he'd find someone else to buy him the horse.

The old man watched his nephew go stalking off.

In his whole life Jamshed had never left the town, had never left the hills to go down to the plains. Not in a car, not in a bus, and certainly not on a horse. Not by the slow blue train either, though every day since he was twenty-five years old he had awaited its arrival in the hope that one of its passengers would choose him to drive them to their hotel, or to one of the town's famous attractions, or better still, to take them on a day-long tour of the sights and visit a few shops.

He had forty-two of the graph-paper exercise books: his current one, and one for each of the last forty-one years of his sixty-two-year-old life. Some were blue and some were green and others were a dusky pink, and in them he'd recorded the big things and the little things; all the events of his days.

He'd recorded how, as a young man, he'd worked as a labourer – felled eucalyptus trees and chopped them into scaffolding and lashed them together and scurried around with wheelbarrows full of gravel and lime, lifted and shovelled until his hands bled, and coughed and blinked with his eyes smarting and tears running down his dusty cheeks.

He'd recorded how, in the evenings in those days, he'd go for a smoke on the uprooted backseat of an Ambassador taxi which lay amongst the mechanical debris of the overflowing courtyard in the repair garage of the Bharat Petroleum Station where his friend Prem spent his life lying on his back or hunched over his own stomach, delving into the broken innards of buses and other people's cars. He'd recorded how Prem, who'd spent four years in English medium school, helped him learn English.

He'd recorded the death of his mother.

The marriage of his brother, Bipin.

The birth of his nephew, Ravi.

The death of his father.

He'd recorded the departure of Prem to Kerala.

The death in a car wreck of his brother, Bipin – Ravi's father – and Bipin's wife, Deesha, Ravi's mother. Ravi going to live with Deesha's sister.

He'd recorded what he'd told his nephew, not once, but many times over the years: that life was hard and full of unexpected calamities, and that all religions were only designed to ease its pain. They were all nonsense, he'd told his nephew again and again, and they were all the same, none of them was any better than any other. They'd all been dragged by people through time, and Ravi was better off without any of them. Better off relying on nothing and no one, better off remembering that he had only one life, this life, and that there was nothing beyond him or outside him. On many different pages, he'd recorded how his nephew seemed to have taken all this to heart, only to become fixated on the notion that he could one day turn himself into a famous Country and Western singer.

Jamshed picked up one of the oldest and most faded of his graph-paper journals and began to read. He read how one evening he'd been sitting on the broken springs of the seat of the Ambassador taxi in the chilly forecourt of the Bharat Petroleum Station, having a smoke with Prem, when the miserable remains of a crashed auto rickshaw had arrived in a cart drawn by a young brown horse and how, for less than the price of a new pair of shoes, he'd bought it.

It was a fine thing, an auto rickshaw.

Nimble and light and shaped like a steam iron to work into the smallest and least friendly of spaces on a busy road. And so many people, all the time, in need of one – the do-gooders from Europe and Scandinavia and North America and Australia who came to volunteer at St Mary's Catholic orphanage and St Peter's Protestant church and the Women Workers' Co-operative; the tourists from everywhere who arrived on the slow blue train, wanting to visit the Botanical Gardens or buy chocolate at the famous King Star Chocolate Shop or have lunch at the Savoy Hotel. And on top of the do-gooders and the tourists there was everyone else – people going to the market, schoolchildren who needed to be ferried to and from school. It was a good place for such a vehicle. He would not have to break his back with a wheelbarrow, his eyes would not sting from the lime, his hands would not bleed from scraping gravel off the ground onto his shovel.

It was all written down on the last graph-paper page in his third book: how Prem helped him take apart all the separate pieces of the vehicle's body that were not already detached from each other, and hammer them out, and patch them. Inside, the engine was small and black like a tiny shrunken heart. It took days to get it going – every time Prem thought he had it, it sputtered to life only to cough and die with a single puff of dirty smoke. 'Try again,' said Jamshed, late one night when they'd been working on it since dawn, 'one last time,' and Prem tried, and the thing breathed and came to life at last. From the market Jamshed bought two pieces of new blue tarpaulin to hang over each side of the open cab to keep out the weather. He attached a green rubber horn he could reach from the driver's seat. He had no idea how to drive but he was sure he would master it, and he'd been certain then, that it would be the beginning of something.

Jamshed closed the old journal and replaced it near the bottom of the pile beneath the others.

He could hardly believe in the coming of Mr Byrd, who since his fall had insisted he would use no other driver. The younger drivers had been envious at first, but their envy had now turned to mirth. They did imitations of Mr Byrd, of his thin height and the way he walked with his nose in the air – Siva on the shoulders of Manoj, Prabhu scuttling in their wake calling, *Sir, please! Botanical Gardens! Lake! Chocolate Shop!*

Well, he didn't care.

'Stupid boys,' he called to them.

15

Byrd had never been to sea, but in three short weeks he'd come to love his bungalow in the presbytery garden the same way he thought a sailor must love his ship. The way the five small rooms all fitted neatly together. The tidy order of everything. The stowing away of his supplies in the orange plastic vegetable stand and the green fridge and on the paper-covered shelves. The arrangement of his books on the windowsills. The feeling of calm he had in the evenings when he came back after a day driving around with the old man, when he'd had dinner with the Padre, or had made himself supper and eaten it and was sitting with a book in the Carter's Nest For Rest, reading, or looking out through the windows over the tops of the trees at the edge of the presbytery garden, towards the tea-covered hills above the town. The mist and the clouds and the rain. High up here by himself, on the slope of this other hill, it was like being in an ark that had come to rest, happily, in this precise spot.

He still had some bad days.

They arrived without warning and he could not get up. Days when he stayed in the three-quarter bed and it seemed impossible that the things that had given him pleasure only yesterday could do so today.

On these days he didn't go down to the concrete steps where the old man, Jamshed, waited for him. He didn't go outside into the presbytery garden or take a stroll up and down the driveway. In the evenings he boiled some rice and mixed in a packet of biryani paste and ate it and went back to bed and hoped for sleep.

On other days when he felt low, but not defeated, he ventured out as usual in the old man's auto, touring the town and talking to him as they drove, and for the most part, he was OK. Most days, in fact, Hilary Byrd felt remarkably cheerful and excited and generally *up*.

It seemed a long time now since he'd arrived; an age since his chance encounter with the Padre on the mountain train; an eternity since his first morning when he'd sat at his table eating the bun he'd bought in Modern Stores (which had turned out, to his surprise, to be pineapple, not banana).

Under the white eaves of the dark red post office, he posted a package to Wyn: a pound of cashew nuts and a packet of local tea, a small bottle of eucalyptus oil, and a letter which he knew would be superseded by his emails, but which he included because it seemed wrong to send a parcel without a letter. She'd been so against him coming, the whole idea of him travelling by himself.

He was much better, he'd written.

And – wait for it, Wyn – I have been clothes shopping.

Yes, I know. Me, clothes shopping!

He explained how when he arrived in the hills he'd been wearing all the wrong things – how ridiculous he'd felt, as well as very cold, stepping off the train in his shorts and his short-sleeved travelling shirt, his Panama hat. Suddenly the lightweight wardrobe that had actually *oppressed* him down on the plains, sticking to his skin like a heavy and uncomfortable shroud, had been ludicrously insubstantial. Down on the plains he'd looked with longing at the men in their breezy sarongs – what his guidebook called their *lungis*. Folding and unfolding them around their legs through the day. But in the mountains, he'd stood on the station platform shivering in his inadequate clothes. The most foolish thing of all was his hat. He'd been torn between keeping it on as a barrier against the drizzle and squashing it into his suitcase. In the end he'd carried it.

Since then the old man, Jamshed, had driven him to a number of different shops where he'd bought a pair of long trousers, two long-sleeved shirts, five pairs of socks, a new pair of sturdy sandals, a waterproof jacket, and a fleece hat. He was warm and well-dressed and properly defended against the weather.

Don't worry about me, Wyn, he'd written, *I'm fine, I really am.*

At the bank, next to the post office, he changed a little more money, and then he went to the library, because he'd made up his mind to educate himself about the place, about the town and its history and how it had come to be what it was. It would be interesting, he thought, to unpick everything that was familiar about it from everything that wasn't. Everything that made him feel as if he could be in Sussex, say, or Kent, from everything that made him feel he was somewhere completely incomprehensible and foreign and strange.

In the reading room he found what seemed to be a suitable book and settled himself into one of the wing-backed chairs. The only sounds were the dry rustling every few minutes of his fingers turning the pages, the ticking of the timbers somewhere in the wall or in the roof space. This, he almost wanted to shout, is what a library should be like! A silent sanctuary, a place of quiet repose and reading and peaceful contemplation and learning! Not the tapping of keyboards and the singing of babies and the hysterical shouting of the drunk and the angry, not the loud show-offy inquiries of the family history folk. Not a place where even the other librarians were noisy. Not a place where, when you told a young woman in a floral dress to please stop zipping and unzipping her backpack she kicked a hole in the counter and told you to go fuck yourself. Not a place where, when you asked an elderly man in an Aran sweater and tweed trousers to please make notes on a pad of paper instead of speaking into a tape recorder, you were called a bald cunt. No. It was none of those things. It was a place to feel calm and cocooned and happy and faraway from the clamour of the world.

His hands had begun to shake. His heart was beating very fast. 'Stop,' he told himself. 'Don't.' He took a few deep breaths. Slowly his heart settled and his hands grew still. 'There,' he said softly. 'Good.'

On the opposite wall, beneath the eaves, a collection of mounted hunting trophies hung above the bookcases: a bear and a leopard, a buffalo with one glass eye missing. Lower down, newspapers were suspended from polished wooden poles, some of them in English, some of them covered in the strange hieroglyphics of languages he couldn't identify or understand but supposed must be Tamil or Hindi, or both. He moved towards them and stood scanning the headlines he could read and those he couldn't. MAN MISTAKEN FOR PIG KILLED, he read.

He went back to his book, read, sank deeper in his chair, slept.

16

With the mattock the Padre used in the garden, Priscilla prised open the bungalow's bedroom window and climbed in. Everything smelled damp because Mr Hilary Byrd had closed all the windows. On the dresser, the brim of his straw hat was floppy with moisture. She put it on and studied herself in the mirror.

She'd never seen him wear it, not even the day he arrived, when she'd returned from town to see him approaching the presbytery along the driveway, tugging his big wheeled suitcase through the puddles – his thin knee-shorts fluttering in the breeze, the hat hanging from his hand, limp and pale. It had struck her then, that very first day, how like a mop he looked: his skinny legs, white as flour and shockingly exposed; his tall body and the pieces of thin, fluffy hair wafting about in the air above his head.

She made her rolling, lopsided way through the small interconnected rooms of the bungalow: out of the bedroom and through the bathroom with its big pink bucket full of Mr Hilary Byrd's washing that he'd put to soak, into the little kitchen with its neat paper-covered shelves and curious assortment of groceries – the porridge and the jam, the Nescafé, the many packets of biryani paste, the silver bags of chocolate. A pan sat on the rear burner of the stove.

She turned into his sitting room. In the corner the green

fridge hummed, a twig popped in the grate though there were no flames.

She sat down in the big comfortable chair in front of the still-warm fire and closed her eyes.

She remembered grasses and thorns and soft pungent wrappings and looking out through a sunlit gap and seeing people walking beside the lake.

It had been her whole world, being in the grasses and the thorns and the wrappings, and looking out through the gap and waiting for food to come. What it signified, everything she could see beyond the gap, she'd had no idea; was it the same world as hers, or a different one?

She'd seen the woman before, walking with the girls along the lake: the tall woman who'd reached in one day and brought her out. The tall woman who was Aunty. Who'd worn a blue sari and a white cardigan that day; Priscilla will never forget it. The soft cardigan, the rustle of the long sari against the grasses and reeds at the edge of the lake. Later, Aunty would tell her that she'd heard the sound of a child; that, like Pharoah's daughter by the bull rushes, she'd seen something hidden in the greenery.

Aunty said the other person who was with Priscilla sometimes in the grasses and thorns, who came and went and brought food, and arranged the wrappings around Priscilla when she left, was likely her mother. That the wrappings had been to hide her, to keep her safe till her mother returned from her business.

'Mine?' Priscilla had asked, wonderingly. '*My* mother?'

Aunty had nodded. They'd looked for her, she said. Some of the older girls had stayed close to the hiding place by the lake and waited for her to return but she didn't come. They'd gone back many times and so had Aunty but she never came. Aunty said they thought that Priscilla's mother was likely a Toda woman, and that she had hidden her while she went off to work. Priscilla, though not tall, had a Toda look about her, said Aunty.

'What work?' Priscilla had asked, but Aunty didn't say. She told Priscilla her mother was a poor woman who likely did what no one should have to do.

Priscilla went back into the kitchen. She ate a spoonful of Hilary Byrd's jam and a square of his chocolate. She read the headlines of the newspapers the Padre had used to line his shelves, some of them new and some of them old – one about the repairs to the east stand at the old racecourse, one about the appointment of a new buildings supervisor from Perth, Australia, at the expensive boarding school in town, and one about the smashing of the oil lamps and some statues on the altar of the Chapel of the Sisters of St Clare in Karnataka.

She walked through into the bedroom where, hanging still from the hook on the back of the door, were the clothes the missionary, Mr Henry Page, had left behind: his dark brown trousers, his red and blue plaid shirt, his hat with the bobble. Above the bed was the embroidered placard which said, *I will be your Shield, your High Tower, the Horn of your Salvation.*

Well.

Still wearing Mr Hilary Byrd's straw hat, she studied herself one last time in the mirror before she took it off and set it down on the dresser where she'd found it. Then she slipped out through the open window, and went back to the presbytery.

17

It had been terrible, trying to talk to Kerrigan in his little ointment-coloured surgery next door, and it was always Kerrigan, somehow, he'd ended up seeing.

Even though their neighbour's practice had expanded over the years – even though Wyn had asked more than once if one of the younger doctors could see her brother this time – it was always Kerrigan who was sitting there with his back to the dark, pink-painted walls when they walked in; Kerrigan asking him to describe his feelings. Perhaps the old doctor thought it was a kindness, but the sight of him, that last time, sitting behind his desk and looking out expectantly from behind his wire-framed glasses, had made Byrd cry. How was it even possible, he'd asked Wyn afterwards through his tears, that Kerrigan was still there after all these years? How old was he? Eighty? A hundred?

Every illness, every setback, in Byrd's life had been investigated beneath the chill circle of Kerrigan's stethoscope moving across his chest, and by the little light which for almost half a century their doctor-neighbour had shone in his eyes and his ears every time he'd ever gone in there. Every prescription that had ever come had arrived across Kerrigan's desk in Kerrigan's unchanging blue-black handwriting and Byrd could not bear, any more, to look at it. The familiar backwards slope of the large, boldly formed letters felt to

Byrd like a part of everything that was wrong. Looking across Kerrigan's desk at Kerrigan, at Kerrigan's mouth opening and closing, and hearing himself being asked to describe his feelings, he couldn't speak. Wyn had taken him over there a dozen times this past year, and in the end, like his Aunt Peggy, he'd refused to go again.

But something about the old auto rickshaw driver's hunched shoulders and occasional brief, softly spoken replies, was soothing, and made him want to talk. Perhaps it helped that he was always speaking to the back of the old man's head as they were driving around – perhaps that made everything easier, he wasn't sure.

In the mornings now, his habits were regular as clockwork. By eight he was up and about and moving around his bungalow, boiling water for a shave and tea. He had not repeated the experience of the sticky pineapple bun for his breakfast: every day since that first one, he'd carried a bowl of porridge to his desk in the long verandah room and eaten it looking out across the presbytery garden and over the tops of the trees, to the hills and the mist on the opposite side of the town. Then he went round checking that all the windows were closed, and at nine, he let himself out through the bungalow's front door and locked it, made his way along the red earth driveway to the road and down the broad concrete steps past the women in the field there, and by 9.15 he was at the bottom of the hill where Jamshed and his yellow auto awaited him.

The order of his day varied, but in general he stopped off at most of the same places: at the Botanical Gardens to stroll beneath the trees; at Modern Stores to do his grocery shopping. At the market, in the little cafe at the south entrance, he bought himself a cup of sweet milky tea and bought his fruit and his vegetables and sometimes a piece of chicken or fish; at the King Star Chocolate Shop he called in for his chocolate, and at the bank when he needed to change a little more money; at the post office and the Global Internet Cafe to send a parcel or an email to Wyn; at the Nazri Hotel for his lunch. After that, if the Assembly Rooms were showing a subtitled English or American film, or a dubbed one he already knew and could follow, he went to that, and from there for an hour or two to the library, to read what he could find about the history of the town, and then it was home to the little mission house for supper and the lighting of a fire; for reading, and for writing to Wyn about the things he'd seen and discovered; about the construction of the town by the British, for example – about the party of British soldiers who, led by a man called John Sullivan from Buckinghamshire, rode up into these mountains on a January day in 1819 prospecting for a suitable location for a military hospital and returned to the plains with the news that they'd come upon a sort of heaven.

They made their way up on horseback, wrote Byrd, *between rocks and trees and a dark kind of jungle, thinking at first that they were on a hiding to nothing, but then after six days of sweltering scrub and forests, they seemed to pass through an invisible wall, and when they came out on the other side everything was suddenly fresh and cool. It was like being at home, they told people when they got back to their barracks on the plains, and it wasn't long before the builders and the engineers arrived and soon there were shops and some houses and a church. A club. The military hospital.*

Soon there was a library, a racecourse, and a hunt (because in the trees, there were jackals and leopards and bears to go after instead of foxes). Large, comfortable houses went up, with fireplaces and tennis courts and flower gardens. Then came the digging of a lake, and finally the railway – the same one that rescued me from the ghastly heat of the plains.

Byrd told Wyn he'd always been aware, of course, that such places existed, high up here in the Indian hills, that the British had built them, and lived in them, and eventually, when the curtain finally came down on the empire, left them. What surprised him, he wrote, was how much he liked it here.

He laid his pen down and looked out across the presbytery garden.

What was it, exactly, that he liked so much? Was it because it had an aura of home, or because it felt completely strange and new?

The fact was, home by itself depressed him. Home made him ill. Home, since leaving the library, had become intolerable. After losing his place in the library, he could hardly bear, any more, to look out into the long thin garden at its high brown fence, its arrangement of shrubs. Even with Wyn there in the evenings and at weekends, being in any of the house's carpeted rooms among the familiar furniture almost overwhelmed him with despair.

In the last few weeks here in the hills, he'd come to enjoy the hectic excitement of the place, the noise and the relentless activity, the colour and sparkle and the glittering untidiness of the streets which every day turned up something surprising – a piece of fried fruit he expected to be sweet but which when he bit into it, wasn't; a pile of dismembered bones and meat in the market he was certain was lamb but which turned out to be chicken.

And yet he wasn't sure if he'd like it as much as he did if it wasn't for the things that *were* like home and therefore made him feel *at* home – the calm orderliness of the Botanical Gardens, for instance, and the Victorian splendour of the old library; the gingerbread eaves of the post office and the piles of Penguin paperback books in Higginbotham's, all in English, most of which he knew like the back of his hand.

Perhaps – he found himself saying to the old man, Jamshed, as they drove through the town and Byrd sat on the floor of the clattering auto just behind him – it was the combination of the strange and familiar that suited him. Perhaps there was a balance that was just right for his personality. Perhaps it provided him with a sort of perfect equilibrium.

'What do you think, Jamshed?'

The old man's head wobbled. It wobbled in that peculiar and exasperating way Byrd had come across in other drivers during his wanderings down on the plains and which he didn't understand – could never tell if it meant *yes* or *no*.

Never mind. It didn't really matter what the old man thought. The important thing was that for some reason Byrd found it easy to talk to him in a way he'd never been able to talk to Kerrigan, or even, this past year, to Wyn.

He stretched his legs out across the floor of the little cab and looked out through the flapping blue tarpaulin that hung over the open side of the vehicle. It was raining again, and a scatter of droplets blew against the edge of the tarpaulin before spraying pleasantly across his face.

It was a terrible thought, that he could still be languishing down there in the heat if he hadn't overheard the Germans talking about the slow blue train; that he might still be lying in his underwear on the bed in his air-conditioned room, unable to venture outside, instead of being here in the soft mild air of this interesting old town, riding around the place in the back of the old man's auto with the Padre's delightful little bungalow to call his own.

18

'Ah yes,' said the Padre, nodding and smiling benignly.

He'd been listening quietly to Hilary Byrd tell him about his afternoon's reading – what he'd discovered about the town's history: about the British soldiers who'd ridden up into the mountains on a January day in 1819 and found a high grassy plateau strewn with mist. A place where they could build a town. 'Like a little corner of England. A place to rest in, out of the heat, and be comfortable and cool.'

The Padre spread his short arms. 'Comfortable and cool, exactly, Mr Byrd, sir! What was it your famous earl said when he came? – "*Such beautiful English rain, such delicious English mud!*"' He lifted his palms to the damp and crumbling ceiling of the presbytery's old dining room, through which, in one far corner, the rain dripped slowly into a cluster of metal and plastic containers on the floor. 'They came for the weather, Mr Byrd – like you. Like *you*, Mr Byrd!'

The Padre popped a bright green fryum in his mouth and tilted his head to one side, and for a moment he sat looking at Hilary Byrd across the table, as if he might be wondering whether anyone, ever, really went anywhere *just* for the weather; if any human being could really be so straightforward, or have such simple needs. Briefly, he seemed to be on the point of saying something, but nothing came, and instead he pushed a dish of Priscilla's light and airy parathas towards his

English visitor, and then Priscilla herself came in to gather their water glasses, and the mostly empty dishes on which the food she had cooked for them had been served.

Byrd had seen her many times now, around the place, since his first dinner with the Padre – usually through the window of the long verandah-like room at the front of his bungalow when he was at his desk reading, or writing to Wyn, or eating his morning porridge. More often than not, he would become aware of some movement at the edge of his vision, and when he looked up, there she'd be, standing at the back door of the presbytery beating a rug against the wall, or making her swift, undulating way across the garden to gather sticks for the boiler, or to hang out an armful of laundry. On Sundays, he'd seen her climb onto the back of the Padre's motorbike and watched the two of them go puttering off to church. And when he came, as he had tonight, and on several other occasions since his arrival, to have dinner with the Padre in the presbytery, she was always present, coming and going between the kitchen and the dining room. While he and the Padre sat and talked, she fried things and boiled things and ferried them back and forth. From his chair, he could see a small stool on which she rested her short right leg while she was busy at the sink.

She appeared to occupy a position somewhere between a housekeeper and a close relative. When the old clergyman spoke to her it was with a kind of brisk affection – 'Priscilla, this is Mr Byrd, who is visiting all the way from Petts Wood UK,' or 'Priscilla, I think Mr Byrd will eat more rice than that.' In reply she would generally nod and say quietly, 'Yes, Uncle.' Of Byrd himself, she seemed extremely shy, and he had the impression she was always anxious, after performing her various tasks around the table, to get back into the kitchen.

Tonight, the last thing she brought out was a plate of cold sliced pineapple for him and the Padre to share. It was icy and delicious, and when they'd finished it, she came again to collect their plates. After that the usual clatter of washing up and putting away began in the kitchen, and the Padre leaned in close to Hilary Byrd and dropped his voice to a confidential whisper.

'Come, Mr Byrd. I want to show you something.'

19

Today after leaving the Chocolate Shop Mr Byrd is telling his story of more and more staying in bed and not getting up.

His story of being fifty one years old and more and more going only two, three days per week to his library in UK where he has been working now for twenty five years. His story of sometimes going only one day and then, none at all.

Jamshed read over what he'd written, looking for errors of spelling and grammar, because even though his words came more easily from his pen than his mouth, they still fell short of what was in his head, all his fluent thoughts. The tall Englishman had spoken at length, both in the morning and then again in the afternoon, about his library back in the UK and how much he hated the new shelves on wheels and the new self-checkout stations and the new Mothers & Toddlers music group and the noisy new librarian called Margaret. He'd spoken about how upset he'd been by the removal of the dictionaries and the small individual wooden tables, and how he'd been sworn at by a young girl in a flowery dress and an old man in a white sweater. He'd spoken about how he hadn't wanted to talk about any of it to anyone, not to his doctor and not even to his sister.

Jamshed closed his journal. He knew he always made

mistakes. The problem was knowing where they were, and in what way, exactly, they were wrong. He tried to conjure Prem's sharp, demanding voice in his head, telling him to go through everything again, to check his tenses and his verb endings and his plurals. To examine his use of the definite and indefinite articles. Reminding him to use 'a' instead of 'one'. Pointing out when to use a double 'l' instead of a single one.

He pictured Mr Byrd again in the back of the auto, leaning forward with his arms on the rail, talking about himself; Mr Byrd who was sometimes so full of excitement and curiosity, and then other times so upset and distressed about the changes at his library back in England.

Mr Byrd's voice trembled when he spoke of these things. Even though he said how much he was enjoying himself here in the hills, there were days when the changes at his library back in England seemed to fill his head completely, and in between visiting his favourite places, he returned to them constantly, like a bag of bones he couldn't help gnawing at, over and over and over. Today, when he'd been talking about it all again, his fingers had closed around the air next to his face and he'd knocked the metallic side of the auto with his empty fist.

Jamshed wished Prem were here. He would have liked so much to talk to Prem about Mr Byrd – to know what he made of the tall Englishman.

Jamshed's own opinion was that Mr Byrd resembled a scarab beetle. A scarab beetle on its back, all its legs and arms waving about, rocking from side to side trying to flip itself the right way up.

20

The trunk was blue and made of tin, like a hundred others Byrd had seen piled up in towers at the market and strapped beneath flapping tarpaulins to the roof racks of buses.

The Padre opened it.

Did Mr Byrd know what it was?

Byrd hesitated. He was fairly sure he did. In spite of the meagre contents he could see inside, he was fairly certain he knew exactly what it was.

'Yes,' said Byrd. His mother and his aunt would have called it a hope chest.

There were some embroidered tablecloths, an electric kettle, a thin roll of cash in a brown rubber band; a white saucer with a small quantity of gold jewellery on it.

'For Priscilla on her wedding day,' said the Padre. 'Whenever I can, I pop something in.'

The two men stood in silence. Byrd didn't know what to say. He had the feeling the Padre was waiting for him to offer up a comment, but he had no idea what the right thing might be. He shifted the position of his feet and replaced, across the top of his head, a loose, thin strand of hair that had flopped out over his ear. He wondered if he was being invited to make a contribution of some sort – a pair of earrings perhaps, or an electric food mixer, or some cash. The price he was paying to stay in the little mission house was very low, far lower than he would have to pay at the Nazri Hotel or the Savoy. The Padre had called it 'the missionary rate'; perhaps, thought Byrd, he was being asked now to pay a little more on top, either in cash or in kind.

Downstairs in the kitchen, he could hear Priscilla stumping about in her big boot.

'When I am gone, Mr Byrd,' the Padre said softly, 'she will have no one.'

Byrd swallowed. He felt the familiar mixture of guilt and anxiety which had so oppressed him when he'd been hustled by the crowds of auto rickshaw drivers down on the plains and on his first day here in the mountains, all of them demanding far more money than he wanted to give. He wondered what kind of thing the Padre had in mind; how little cash he could offer, how inexpensive a gift, without appearing mean. No doubt the Padre thought of him as a wealthy man – no doubt everyone here thought the tourists who came were rich as Croesus, but Hilary Byrd did not feel rich. No decision had yet been reached with the library about him taking his pension early; his only funds were his modest savings and the envelope of cash Wyn had pressed on him at the airport.

He wished Wyn was with him. Wyn would know what to say and what to give and how to deal lightly and easily with the situation. He looked down at his feet. The words from his guidebook came back to him. *Do not make eye contact. If you make eye contact you are lost.*

'Padre –' he began uncertainly and without looking up, but the Padre interrupted him with a sigh. 'A year ago, Mr Byrd, I thought I had found someone. But it was not to be.'

After that the Padre stood for what seemed like a long

moment, gazing down into the chest at the kettle and table-cloths, the roll of money and the saucer of jewellery, as if willing them to proliferate in a magical way. Byrd was relieved when at last the old clergyman reached for the edge of the lid and pulled it shut and said, 'Come, Mr Byrd, it is late. You must be tired and wanting your bed.'

21

On Tuesdays and Thursdays after he finished at the CTR Salon, the old driver's nephew, Ravi, went to the house of Miss Moreland, the Australian organist from St Peter's (the one who so annoyed the Padre by playing a steady two beats behind the singing congregation) and swept the fallen eucalyptus leaves from her driveway and lawn and from the old lichen-covered tennis court at the back of her house.

Inside the garage door there was a short-handled brush, and Ravi went up and down the drive with it, clearing the leaves and twigs that fell from the overhanging trees and made the ground slippery and untidy. Sometimes, on the old tennis court, he played a few strokes with the brush, thwacking a pine cone over the sunken, crusted net. Maybe when he was settled in Chennai he would take up tennis. Get himself a white outfit like they wore at Wimbledon, or something slinky in a bright colour like they preferred at the American Open. Often, between clients at the CTR Salon, he watched the tennis when it was on TV. Once, sweeping Miss Moreland's court, he'd found the remains of an old racquet buried in the ground where the baseline, if there'd still been one, would have been. He'd thought at first it was an old bone, something speckled and grey from an animal's shoulder or jaw, but when he lifted it out he saw a mesh of stiff, misshapen strings, more like a fishing net than anything you would try to hit a ball with.

He'd presented it to Miss Moreland, who said, 'Oh goodness, Ravi, it must have been lying there for half a century or more.' No doubt it had belonged to her great-aunt, she said. Her great-aunt had lived here a long time ago. She was English, said Miss Moreland, and travelled here by ship from Southampton in 1898 with her parents and her sister, who was Miss Moreland's grandmother. 'Her father was involved in some capacity with the railway. She grew up to be the librarian here. Yes. It's why the house is so full of books. She was a great reader. I have a photograph of her. She was a famous figure in the town, a large woman in brown brogues and an aertex shirt who rode a bicycle. She doesn't ever seem to have felt the cold.' Miss Moreland had never spoken before to Ravi at such length. She turned the old tennis racquet with its perished strings over in her hands and her voice became dreamy. 'The house found its way to me eventually and I decided to come and live in it.' For a few moments she stood silently, looking up at the house. She had forgotten, perhaps, that Ravi was still there. 'Her name was Elspeth. She was happy here. I thought I might be too.'

Two years ago, with the money Miss Moreland paid him, Ravi had bought the white Stetson.

Everything else – the fringed waistcoat, the piebald chaps, the blue and white checked shirt with the piped red yoke, the pair of pointy silver-toed cowboy boots, the guitar – his uncle had paid for since he started driving the tall Englishman around.

All he needed, now, was the horse.

22

It came to Byrd in the middle of the night.

The rain had arrived again and he could hear the plock-plock of water on the boiler house roof. He had been sleeping and now he was awake.

She likes you.

It was as if he was in the garden again, the day the Padre had ambushed him from behind the hydrangea bush with the rusty secateurs, only this time the scene seemed to have merged in his mind with the one from a few hours ago when he was standing beside the old clergyman in front of the hope chest in the little bedroom upstairs at the back of the presbytery, and now, when he replayed it, he was certain that the Padre had not been talking about the dog.

The middle of the night was always Byrd's worst time. In the hours between two and four, he almost always woke feeling anxious, and as he lay listening to the rain on the boiler house roof, his most recent encounter with the Padre kept coming back to him.

A year ago I thought I had found someone but it was not to be.

Priscilla clumping about downstairs in her big boot.

When I am gone, Mr Byrd, she will have no one.

Byrd lay with his eyes open. On the opposite wall a stripe of moonlight fell across the embroidered placard which hung there. *I will be your Shield, your High Tower, the Horn of your Salvation.*

Oh dear no.

He pushed back his quilt and swung his bare feet onto the linoleum floor.

He went to the window of the verandah room and looked out. Beneath the night sky the pale flowers in the garden shone but the presbytery was dark and the black dog was asleep in her sink.

In his kitchen he struck a match and lit the gas on the Ideal Pigeon stove and boiled water for some tea. In the half-dark the blue flame burned.

Was it possible the Padre considered that he, Hilary Byrd, might volunteer to take Priscilla off his hands? Had the old clergyman spotted him on the platform at Mettupalayam that day and thought, 'There. That tall thin man sweating beneath his Panama hat who looks exhausted and unwell – maybe that is the man I have been looking for. Yes. Maybe him.' Had the Padre climbed into the same compartment on purpose? Had he, with his friendly smile and his snowman's scarf and his offer of cheap accommodation, deliberately stalked him?

Byrd tried to recall the details of his train journey into the mountains.

He remembered they'd exchanged a few words about the view: about the bright, clipped patterns of the tea plantations, and the fields of carrots divided into raised beds, like fresh graves; that they'd laughed together at the small grey monkeys playing and foraging in heaps of rubbish beside the track. He remembered that when they reached Coonoor and the air had suddenly cooled and he'd said, 'Thank God!', the Padre had asked, 'What brings you here, Mr Byrd, up into the hills?'

He pictured the two of them last night, bent over the open hope chest.

When I am gone she will have no one.

Byrd closed his eyes and let go of a small groan. How embarrassing.

He drank his tea.

He went back to bed and tried to read but he couldn't. He flipped open book after book, the memoirs by Stendhal and Gide and Flaubert, his Chekhov and his Thomas Mann, and closed them all without taking in a single word. He felt as if something had been stolen from him – the missionary's bungalow had felt like a gift, a sanctuary away from everything in his life that frightened him or made him sad; it had felt like a cosy sort of refuge here in this interesting and attractive little town where for some reason he felt better than he had in a long time.

At five, he got up again and made more tea and drank it sitting in front of the fireplace in the Carter's Nest For Rest. From the forest came the strange bird-like cry the Padre told him was the sound of a barking deer. Outside a scrim of cloud hung in a palely illuminated sky above the hilltops. The trees were dark and still. He could see the black dog sleeping in her sink.

Oof.

He hated conflict; shrank from awkward and uncomfortable situations. Wyn was always the one to deal with any unpleasantness with the bank or the utility companies. Wyn was the one who, years ago, had written to the university examination board to ask permission to sit with her brother while he took his finals – had explained that without her there, he would most likely be unable to complete them. She was the one who'd gone to the library and sat down with Margaret to begin the paperwork connected with his leaving.

He got up out of the big chair and rubbed his face with his hands.

It was fully light outside now, and he wondered if perhaps, in those awful dangerous hours of the night between two and four, he'd managed to get the wrong end of the stick. Was that possible? Through the open door into the verandah room he saw another of the embroidered placards that decorated the bungalow's painted walls. *Lean Not On Thine Own Understanding.*

Could he have misunderstood things?

He went back to the window and looked out across the sleeping garden.

Well, he would hang on, at least for a little while, and hope nothing embarrassing occurred. He'd carry on doing what he'd been doing except perhaps he wouldn't have dinner quite so often at the presbytery. Today he'd go to the lake as he'd planned and then after lunch to the lovely quiet library, and if things did become awkward with the Padre – well, he would just tell him, in the politest possible way, that he had no plans, at his age, to marry; that he'd been ill and had only come here to recuperate.

23

'No, boy!'

'Please, Uncle!'

The horse Ravi wanted to buy belonged to the cousin of the manager of the shop at the Bharat Petroleum Station. He had seen it one day, clopping slowly across the forecourt between a line of white taxis and a Hillmaster bus loaded with schoolchildren, and now its owner had agreed to sell it to him.

It was thin and it had a wound of some kind high up on its thigh, and the price was no more than his uncle made in a few weeks driving the skinny Englishman.

'Uncle, please.'

'No! No horses. Anyway look, this horse is at death's door. Hole in leg. No, boy.'

What Jamshed had brought with him today and had purchased with the money he'd made driving Hilary Byrd since the buying of the cowboy boots and the piebald chaps, the waistcoat, the jeans, the shirt and the bootlace tie, was a spare guitar. A spare guitar in case the other one broke, which Ravi said happened all the time, with guitars.

'Here, boy,' said Jamshed. 'In case of accident.'

Ravi said thank you. He looked sheepish and a little shame-faced and for a minute or two he strummed happily on the new instrument. Then he brought up the horse again. He had set his heart on it, he said. It was part of the whole thing, the horse. His whole dream.

The old man clucked his tongue and shook his head, which made Ravi jump up and practically throw down the guitar.

'Uncle!'

The boy spun away from Jamshed on the sloping heels of his brand new cowboy boots. The horse was important! he burst out. The horse would make him special, different from any other Country and Western singers there might be in the cities. He looked close to tears. He'd go crazy, he shouted, if he was still at the hair salon five years from now. Ten years, twenty years. He'd go crazy if he was living in a hut by the river when he was an old man wearing one black flip-flip and one red plastic clog and a stupid short-sleeved shirt that said WORLD CLASS on his back. He would drown himself in the lake, he said, if he never got the chance to do something with his life.

The old man was silent.

He looked down at his feet. If he was stung by the boy's outburst, he didn't show it. He didn't say that if it hadn't been for the boy's costume and the money he was saving to give to him, he'd have bought himself a couple of shirts and a new pair of shoes by now. He toed the wet dust. A damp wind blew, and beyond the river the pine trees snapped.

For a long time he didn't speak or look at his nephew. He wanted Ravi to make something of himself. He really did. He just wasn't sure about the whole Country and Western thing. It seemed like a terrible idea. As far as he could tell, the boy could barely play the guitar. He patted his nephew's shoulder, caught again between wanting to help him and thinking he should do everything he could to try and change his mind. He shook his head; dipped his hand into the pocket of his trousers and brought out his wallet.

'Here, boy,' he said quietly. 'For horse.'

24

In the morning, after his sleepless night, Byrd went, as planned, to the lake and rented a rowing boat while the old driver, Jamshed, waited for him at the kerb next to the ticket kiosk.

On his way out from the presbytery he'd seen neither the Padre nor Priscilla; only the dog, Ooly, had been there in her sink when he exited his bungalow, looking up at him with her peculiar expression of love, longing, and sorrowful reproach.

Out on the lake, he rowed himself inexpertly about, doing his best not to think about the previous evening upstairs in the bedroom with the Padre and the hope chest, and when he did, to tell himself it was nothing, only a ridiculous idea that had come to him because he'd woken in the middle of the night.

At noon he went to the Nazri Hotel for lunch and now he was in the reading room at the old library, reading about the development of the town under the British, and about the Toda people, who'd been here in the mountains before them: tall, shawled folk who revered the buffalo and forbade themselves shoes or any type of foot covering – folk whose high priest, according to James George Frazer, in the green linen-covered edition of *The Golden Bough* Byrd pulled from the shelf, was called the 'The Sacred Milkman'.

It was a lonely-sounding occupation, thought Byrd, being the Todas' Milkman, in charge of the sacred dairy herd. Like his fellow Todas, the Milkman was not allowed to wear shoes, but things were even harder for him because he was not allowed to cross bridges either (if he came to a river, he had to wade or swim), and had to live in a little hut by himself, far away from all the other Todas, tending to the sacred animals. If he had a wife before being chosen as the Milkman, he had to give her up; children, as well as shoes and bridges, were forbidden to him.

Byrd paused with his finger in the gutter of the book and looked out through the tall many-paned windows of the library at the thick curtain of eucalyptus trees beyond the glass. He was moved by the lonely situation of the Milkman, this solitary individual without shoes and only the big warm bodies of the buffalo and the sweet smell of their sacred milk to keep him company; moved, and at the same time amazed, at the sorts of lives people lived because of their beliefs. What a strange and mysterious thing faith was, to persist in the midst of such odd and arbitrary prescriptions! It was beyond him, how any of the world's religions managed to endure when they were steeped in such silliness. He'd abandoned his own so long ago he could no longer remember how it felt, not to think of it all as nonsense. Of God, for example, in the Book of Genesis, preferring Abel's gift of meat to Cain's of vegetables, which made as little sense, as far as he could see, as the Todas' denying themselves shoes and bridges.

Byrd tilted his head back and looked up at the mangy buffalo head mounted on the wall above his chair and wondered how it had ended up there – if it had been shot by the British hunt, and stuffed, and put up on the wall like a picture; if the Sacred Milkman had felt moved to leave his lonely hut and wade through rivers in his bare feet in order to walk into the office of Mr John Sullivan from Buckinghamshire and remind him that all buffalo were sacred to the Toda people whose home this was before the British came and established their Assembly Rooms and their Botanical Gardens and their railway, their churches and their hospitals and their schools, their grocery stores and their bookshop, their library and their racecourse and their hunt.

Looking up at the buffalo, with its worn and rotted fur and its one glass eye, Byrd wondered how much of a fuss the Milkman might have made, and what John Sullivan might have said by way of a reply. He wondered if there'd been any sort of fight, or trouble.

He sat with the book open in his lap, drowsy in the pale sunlight which had been warmed by its passage through the tall glass windows; sleepy after his night roaming around his bungalow making cups of tea and sitting in the big old chair in front of the fireplace, worrying that the Padre was thinking of him as a possible husband for Priscilla.

His eyes travelled along the shelves, the spines of the thousands of books.

What a vast amount he didn't know!

The thought was always crushing, and on his way home to the presbytery in Jamshed's auto, sitting on the floor behind the old man, he tried to explain how paralysed he felt by that – the thought of all the knowledge he didn't have, and would never have.

Last winter, he told the old man, when he was at home after leaving the library, and Wyn had come again to be with him in the old house, he'd tried to make the feeling go away by learning Chinese.

'Yes, sir,' said Jamshed, pulling out into the traffic.

It was Wyn's idea, said Byrd, and for three months he'd attended classes on Tuesday evenings with a Miss Yu at the Adult College in Beckenham.

'There were thirty of us, men and women of various ages, and Miss Yu promised us that with as few as 2,000 characters we'd be able to read a simple newspaper, but after three months none of us had mastered more than a hundred and fifty and soon I was the only one who hadn't dropped out.'

Sometimes, Byrd told Jamshed, Miss Yu laughed at his pronunciation, which was a little irritating. Still, he'd looked forward to the lessons. He'd found it easier to get up in the mornings, and he could see that Wyn was relieved, less worried about leaving him alone in the house when she went off to work. Then, after the Christmas break, he arrived as usual for the start of class. He'd studied over the holiday and was excited to show Miss Yu what he'd learned. He was quite hoping there might be a test. He'd revised all the numbers from sixty to a hundred; the eight different prepositions they'd covered; the various words meaning 'an amount of' which you need to put before different objects and which change depending on what the object is.

'Sounds difficult, sir,' said the old man.

'It was, Jamshed. It is. It's an extremely difficult language.'

Wyn, said Byrd, had given him presents to give to Miss Yu to celebrate the New Year: one amount of sheepskin slippers and two amounts of left-over Christmas cake. He'd also brought along four amounts of mince pies he'd made himself, but Miss Yu never came. The next morning Wyn phoned the college and was told the class had been cancelled because he was the only one who'd registered for the coming session, and Miss Yu had gone back to China.

Byrd eased himself up off the floor and, stooping beneath the low ceiling of the clattering auto, shuffled backwards onto the leatherette seat and sat without speaking. He'd been very low after the failure of the Chinese classes. Wyn couldn't persuade him to come down for supper in the evenings when she came home from work. She couldn't persuade him to go out with her for a few hours at the weekend, up to London or into Bromley, or to Chislehurst caves for a walk, or to Eltham Palace for a stroll in the grounds. She couldn't persuade him to cook or bake or play Scrabble. She'd even suggested he get the old Singer out and make some new curtains for the sitting room but he'd said no, he had no wish to bake or sew or play Scrabble or do anything.

Eventually she'd suggested Russian classes. The Adult College, she was fairly sure, offered Russian.

'So I took up Russian, Jamshed. I went back to the Adult College and joined a class of men who'd met their Russian wives working in the oil business in Siberia, and we had a teacher called Sergei who came from a small village outside Kiev and lived with his Scottish wife in Croydon.'

Byrd was crouching on the floor again, close to the old driver's head so he could be heard above the hubbub of the traffic.

He'd been very hopeful, he said, that the Russian would give him a sense of purpose and keep his feelings of hopelessness and paralysis at bay. He'd been feeling sick almost all the time and finding the familiar surroundings of his house more and more intolerable. He'd thought he would start to feel better after leaving the library, but he hadn't. There were times when the sense of his own pointlessness descended on him with such overwhelming force he could hardly breathe. He blew out his cheeks, as if he were re-living the experience of being so overwhelmed by his own pointlessness he could hardly breathe, as if he were fighting, even now, for air. He rubbed his temples and gave his head a shake. 'Did you know, Jamshed, that in Russian the verb "to be" is omitted in the present tense? Isn't that strange?'

The old driver observed that verbs were often strange, and that the present tense in English was very difficult. His old friend Prem was always correcting his use of the present tense, he said, but Hilary Byrd wasn't listening. 'I enjoyed the Russian,' he went on, 'while it lasted. We learned to tell the time and ask each other the date and the day of the week and practised losing our passports and identity papers and our luggage. We asked directions and read aloud all the various signs in the picture in the textbook of the Arrivals terminal at Sheremetyevo airport. *Toilets. No Smoking. Lost Property. Way In. Way Out.*'

Byrd gazed out through the open gap in the side of the auto rickshaw and fell silent again. It had made the skin on his scalp prickle to be able to see the word Чехов and know that it meant Chekhov. Feeling a key to something in his hand, he'd loved that.

'You know Chekhov, Jamshed?'

'No, sir.'

'Well you should give him a try. He's very good. I'm sure they'd have something at Higginbotham's. Maybe a translation into Hindi.'

Jamshed did not say that the language he spoke when he was not speaking English – or the smattering of French and German and Japanese he'd picked up over the years from all the tourists and volunteers he'd driven around – was not Hindi, but Tamil. He thought about saying so, but it seemed rude to point out Mr Byrd's mistake.

Suddenly Jamshed swerved to avoid a scooter turning left across their path and Byrd cried out.

'Sorry, sir!' said Jamshed. 'Sorry, sorry, sorry!' but Byrd only flapped his hand. He was used, by now, to the traffic. 'That's all right, Jamshed,' he said. 'I have every confidence you won't kill me.'

After that they rode in silence and Byrd didn't speak again as they made their way up the long hill from the centre of town.

Slowly the old man's tiny vehicle bumped in through the presbytery's gateless entrance, past the plastic sign that said DOG IS ON DUTY, and along the cratered red driveway.

Through the lighted window of the shabby drawing room Byrd could see the Padre, writing at his desk. Somewhere in the back, he supposed, Priscilla would be chopping vegetables.

Butterflies stirred again in the pit of his stomach. He had almost managed to forget about her. Part of him wanted to stay in the old man's auto and not have to get out and for a moment he hesitated.

'Well – goodnight, Jamshed. I'll see you tomorrow.'

'Tomorrow. Yes, sir. Goodnight, sir.'

Byrd walked briskly across the garden to the steps next to the boiler house that led up to his bungalow, keeping his head down. If the old clergyman spotted him and came out and issued an invitation for dinner, he would plead an upset stomach.

He put the key in the lock of the bungalow door; paused. There was a presence just behind him, softly breathing and expectant. He turned the key in the lock and extracted it, bracing himself for the Padre's smiling snowman's face, but when he turned it was only the dog, looking up at him with dark, imploring eyes.

Byrd shook his head.

'No,' he said sternly.

When she didn't move he opened the door only enough so that he could squeeze through the gap without her following.

'Now go,' he ordered, poking his head out through the narrow opening and pointing the way back to her sink. 'And don't come back. I don't want you.'

Inside he sat down heavily in the Carter's Nest For Rest. Through the windows of the verandah room he could see out across the garden, the roses and the asters and the rhubarb, the banana tree and the strange plastic-looking shrub whose name he didn't know, and a great wave of emotion washed over him – a feeling that seemed to contain both happiness and anxiety, a feeling that he was at home here, and also that he wasn't; a feeling that he belonged, somehow, here in these foreign hills, and also that he didn't; a feeling that he was supposed to be here and that he wasn't; that there was a point to everything, and that there was no point at all.

25

They met on the platform at Mettupalayam, the Padre will tell the superintendent of police.

They shared a train compartment, he will say. Mr Byrd looked like someone who was very tired, perhaps not entirely well. 'I was worried about him. He seemed like someone who was in need.'

He was very struck by the Englishman's appearance, he'll say – by the flimsy, flyaway softness of what remained of his hair, and by his long, sad face; by his unsuitable clothes as he headed into the mountains – the combination of his straw hat and his knee-shorts, the large boat-like sandals. By his unwieldy hard-sided suitcase which he manoeuvred as if it contained a pile of rocks. By the aura he gave off of having brought all the wrong things, of being poorly equipped for whatever adventure he was embarked upon; of being, somehow, unmoored.

'He seemed,' the Padre will say, pausing, as if searching how to describe exactly the impression Hilary Byrd had made on him that day, 'lost.'

26

Something is wrong with Mr Byrd, wrote Jamshed.
He is not so bright and cheery as in the beginning, after his fall.

All the way back to the presbytery from the library, Mr Byrd had sat leaning forward with his arms on the rail in front of his seat. In a rapid, rushing voice he'd spoken over the noisy clatter of the auto and the rumble of the traffic, and after that, for a long time, all the way up the steep hill to the presbytery, he'd sat on the back seat without talking. What was the matter with him?

In the beginning, in the weeks after his fall, there'd been some days, it was true, when Mr Byrd had been gloomy and said very little, or spoken unhappily about his life. But on the whole, it seemed to Jamshed, he'd been in good spirits most of the time. Almost every day he said how much he was liking it here in these foreign hills – how much he was enjoying being away from home, from the depressing brown fence and familiar carpets of his house and the noisy unhelpful new librarian called Margaret and his useless doctor called Richard Kerrigan. He said that he was missing his sister but he was liking the drizzling weather and the chocolate shop and the Assembly Rooms and the gardens full of trees and plants and all the old buildings, especially the library. He said he was enjoying the friendly Padre and the comfortable little mission house and the good cooking of the Padre's young housekeeper called Priscilla.

And now Mr Byrd seemed agitated and unhappy. Jamshed didn't know what to make of it. Overnight Mr Byrd had become nervous and distressed and there was a small vibrating twitch under the corner of his left eye which had not been there before.

They were rattling along, now, in the middle of the Mysore Road, below the Savoy Hotel. Hilary Byrd sat with his eyes closed. 'I never wanted to go to school, Jamshed,' he announced suddenly. 'All I wanted to do was to stay at home and read and watch television and play in the garden and go for walks and bake cakes and sew.'

Jamshed nodded. He could see Mr Byrd in the rear-view mirror. They passed in front of Modern Stores and the Assembly Rooms, and the old man watched his English passenger looking mournfully out at the fast-moving traffic and the busy town through the gap in the tarpaulin. Mr Byrd looked as if he was thinking about all the reading and playing and walking and watching television and sewing and baking he could have done instead of being made to go to school.

'My Aunt Peggy used to say it made a difference if you were born in the summer or the winter – into the sunshine or into the dark. Do you think there might be something in that, Jamshed? She and I were both November.'

When Jamshed said he didn't know, that he himself had been born in July, which was both sunny and overcast, Byrd continued: 'When Wyn and I were small, our Aunt Peggy was always disappearing for what our mother called "a rest". We didn't know what it meant at the time though of course I do now.'

He fell into one his brooding silences then, with that look of his which suggested to Jamshed that he might be replaying the whole of his life in his head. They trundled past the chocolate shop, and for a long time Hilary Byrd sat without speaking.

At the market he climbed out and came back with a bag of plums which he started eating quickly, one after another, catching the stones in his palm.

'I should have been more like Coriolanus!' he burst out suddenly.

'Sir?'

'In Shakespeare, Jamshed. The Roman general, Coriolanus. His people tell him they've decided to banish him, but he says, "No! *I* banish *you*!"'

Hilary Byrd let go of a short, wistful laugh.

Yes, he said. He wished now that he'd expressed his feelings when people had started coming to the library to hold jewellery-making demonstrations and musical concerts or to receive help with their job applications. He wished, when they'd come wanting to sit in the new armchairs and chat to each other in what had once been the local history archive, that he'd stood at the door and barred their way and told them they were banished – that he felt about them the way Coriolanus felt about his people – 'that I hated their breath like the reek of rotted fens, Jamshed! Like the dead carcasses of unburied men that did corrupt my air! That I despised them!'

Banishing them, yes! He would have enjoyed that. It would have been dignified and satisfying.

'But I didn't, Jamshed,' he said quietly.

In the car park his sister had held him for a long time. She hadn't told him it didn't matter, because Wyn always knew that it did. He had phoned her in tears. The mothers and toddlers had begun to sing again, and he'd been looking for the poetry shelves but they'd been moved for the third time in a week, and he didn't know where to find them. 'She drove me home, Jamshed, and after that she didn't leave me again for a long time. She went up to her flat in Shepherd's Bush to get her things and moved into our Aunt Peggy's old bedroom and stayed with me in the old house.'

'Petts Wood, sir?'

'That's right, Jamshed. Where we grew up. I've never left it. When I was well enough to be by myself, she went back to work, but she came home in the evenings, and she was there at the weekends too, always.

'What frightened me, Jamshed, was how exhausted she seemed. She'd always had her own way of helping me, but this time she seemed, oh I don't know' – Byrd shrugged and blinked and the old driver heard his voice click and break – 'at a loss.'

Byrd had finished his plums.

'I didn't tell her till the day before. I made all the arrangements while she was at work. It felt like a life-time since I'd done anything for myself. It was the only thing I could think of – to take myself away. To try being *elsewhere*. I convinced myself that being anywhere but *here* – there, I mean, where I was – would be easier. I thought maybe I'd try one of the old Eastern bloc countries, Romania or Slovakia. Then I thought somewhere further away might be better, New Zealand, or South America. I really didn't know where to choose. In the end I came here because – oh I'm not really sure, Jamshed. I suppose I thought there might be more to see, and that, well, I don't know, I thought it might be cheaper, too, than all those other places.'

Mr Byrd was speaking very quietly now, in a kind of murmur Jamshed struggled to hear, 'Wyn was very against it of course. She didn't say so, but she was. Even though she was exhausted and at a loss, I know she thought it was a bad idea – that I wasn't well enough to go anywhere by myself. She said why didn't I wait until September when she could take some time off and we could travel together? But I said I didn't think I could wait for September. I told her I'd write, and email, so she'd know I was OK.'

27

'Mr Byrd!'

The Padre seemed to have materialised out of nowhere. One minute Byrd was walking across the empty garden towards the driveway on his way into town, the next moment the Padre, wrapped up in his scarf and his too-large fleece hat, was moving towards him, his arm raised like a flag.

'Mr Byrd,' he said, a little breathlessly, 'there is something I wish to ask you. A favour. A boon.'

The old clergyman's face was lit with a hopeful-looking smile. His dark eyes were moist, and there was a pleading depth to them that reminded Byrd of the dog's.

Byrd swallowed. He felt himself shrinking and wanting to run away.

'Priscilla –' began the Padre. He glanced furtively at the back door of the presbytery as if he was afraid Priscilla herself might suddenly appear and start beating a rug against the wall or picking up sticks to feed the boiler.

He lowered his voice and took a step towards Hilary Byrd. 'I was hoping, Mr Byrd –'

Byrd took a step backwards. He couldn't help it. *Keep everything light,* he told himself. *Be courteous and polite and it will be quickly over and then forgotten.*

'I was hoping you might be willing to help Priscilla a little with her English. With her reading and her writing? I would do it myself only I am snowed under with my ministry and my accounts.'

Byrd opened his mouth to speak but no words came out. It was not what he'd been expecting. Even so, he was fairly sure this was something he didn't want to do, and he wished for the courage, now, to say no, he was very sorry but he was too busy to help Priscilla with her English.

'I would be very grateful to you, Mr Byrd.'

The dog, Byrd noticed, had joined them and was also, now, looking up at him beseechingly.

'Half an hour in the evenings perhaps, Mr Byrd, sir? If you could spare it?'

28

It had been so quiet at the presbytery, said the Padre to his dead wife. So uneventful with Mr Page gone back to Canada to see about his visa, instead of being busy about the place with his good works. No Mr Page helping him and Priscilla to see to the beggars who came to the entrance asking for rice or eggs or dal or anything else that could be spared; no Mr Page hopping onto the back of the church two-wheeler and going with him into town at night to distribute blankets and buns to the hungry and the homeless, no Mr Page jogging back across the garden after a day at the leper colony.

Yes, said the Padre, popping a pink fryum into his mouth and crunching on it, life had been a little dull without the young missionary, but then, with the rains, Mr Hilary Byrd had come, all the way from Petts Wood UK, and everything now was lively and jolly.

Even Ooly seemed better – more alert and interested in the world, and so amusingly attached to the tall Englishman. 'Even though Mr Byrd,' chuckled the Padre, 'wants nothing to do with her!'

As for Priscilla, he told his wife, she seemed happier too. Priscilla seemed in fine spirits these days.

'With any luck, Vallie, it will only, now, be a matter of time.'

29

At Higginbotham's bookshop, Byrd bought pencils and pens and a soft, maroon cardboard exercise book with graph-paper pages so Priscilla could practise her handwriting. From the library he borrowed a collection of Andersen's fairy tales with pictures and a few lines of simple text on each page, and hoped Priscilla would not be embarrassed, at her age, whatever that was exactly, to be reading to him in her slow halting way from books that were made for children.

At the first lesson he tried her with a few simple sentences he'd prepared himself, in his own handwriting, to see how much she did and didn't know. He picked out a couple of paragraphs of easy text and asked her to read them to him aloud, and it came to him almost immediately, in the first few minutes, that everything was, in fact, all right.

When they sat down together at the Padre's desk with the handwritten pages between them, he glimpsed the two of them, Priscilla and himself, in the wide, speckled mirror of the presbytery drawing room, and he saw a picture of a young woman and a fifty-year-old man; a teacher and his pupil; the Padre working silently in the corner on the church accounts, a yellow legal pad on his knees. The old clergyman wasn't looking at them. There was an ordinary calm to everything, and in the mirror's cloudy silvering, he saw that it was all exactly as it seemed, no more and no less: the Padre had asked him for his help in this small and unexceptional way, and now he was giving it. He'd been foolish to whip himself up into such a state of anxiety about the hope chest and the Padre's wistful remarks and all that they'd appeared, at two-thirty in the morning, to suggest.

The relief!

He almost laughed out loud – no longer worried that the dinners the Padre invited him to at the presbytery three or four times a week were part of some crazy, cunning plot.

He stopped fretting that he would have to leave.

And the teaching, when he got down to it, was fun. There'd been a time, in his twenties, when he'd thought he might have it in him, to become a teacher, of French or German perhaps, or English literature, and he'd wondered over the years if it might have moulded him differently – if it would have made him more resilient and flexible, more accustomed to opposition, braver. But at the time it had terrified him, the idea of twenty or thirty faces tilted up to his, waiting for him to speak; the prospect of them breaking into uproar. Children, the young, had such a keen nose for fear and frailty in others; he remembered that from his own schooldays.

At the library in town he was delighted to find, along with the fairy tales, an assortment of Ladybird books like the ones they'd had at home.

Do we still have them? he wrote to Wyn, tapping excitedly on a grimy keyboard in the Global Internet Cafe. *Up in the attic somewhere? I'd forgotten how good they were – simple but full of useful information and quite entertaining too.*

30

She'd had another name once but could no longer remember it.

Priscilla, Aunty told her, was a joyful name which swept away all the sorrows of her life when she was hidden in the undergrowth before she was found. It was a fine Christian name, she said. 'It means you will live a long life.'

At Aunty's place there'd been a flat upstairs where Aunty lived; a concrete balcony where the girls hung their wet clothes to dry after they'd washed them in the big tub in the yard on Saturdays; a dormitory with six beds for the big girls; a dormitory with six beds for the little girls; an apartment with two beds and a cooking ring for the volunteers who came from the UK and Australia and France and many other countries, who stayed for a few months and then vanished and were never heard from again. There was also a kitchen, and a big room where the girls did their homework and where Aunty gathered them together before they went to bed to sing hymns and say prayers – prayers for things they needed, such as money for school fees and a washing machine and a summer outing; prayers for patience with the government officials who kept coming with new regulations about how Aunty should run her house; prayers for Priscilla to grow some teeth.

For a while, Priscilla had been one of the little girls. She held their hands (except for Smitha's because Smitha did not want to hold a hand without a thumb), and walked with them to school and to St Peter's church. It was always Aunty's hope that money would be found to send them all to St Cecilia's English medium school; in the meantime she had them come to her in the evenings for ten minutes each. There had once been a gift from one of the volunteers of a supply of Ladybird books, and Aunty used these to teach them the precious English language which would be such an advantage to them when the time came to make their way in the world. Thus they were instructed in *What to look for in Summer* and the life of Julius Caesar; in the adventures of Puss in Boots and Sir Walter Raleigh; in *The Weather* and *The Frog Prince,* and many other things, and some of the girls got on quite well but Priscilla was not one of them. The prospect of her ten minutes with Aunty made Priscilla sick with anxiety, and she invented every excuse she could to miss it. Sometimes she told Aunty she had a pain in her left eye and she couldn't see properly; sometimes that she had been chosen (not true) to recite a poem tomorrow in class and must spend all evening learning it.

When Priscilla had been in the big girls' dormitory for some time, Aunty took in the first boy: a small, silent three-year-old from the leper colony. He was healthy but both parents had the disease and they had asked and begged, and in the end the boy had wound up on Aunty's doorstep. 'I don't take boys,' she'd said, but she'd been so moved by the sight of this small silent one whose name was Prabhu that she said, 'Well, all right,' and turned the storeroom into a third dormitory, for boys. And after that, they'd had boys, most of them little ones like Prabhu but also a handful of older ones, and Priscilla noticed that these boys electrified Aunty's calm and ordered household. She also noticed that she was outside this charged and excited atmosphere of electrification, that no eyes followed her when she stumped in from school, no hand tried to nudge hers when they helped themselves to rice and dal and the bowl of wrapped sweets that came out on Sundays. She made herself, therefore, into the person who helped Aunty more than any of the others with the cooking.

And then one day a man came from the government. He ate dinner with Aunty. Aunty sat up tall with her arms folded and shouted more than usual. 'Bring Sir two double-fried eggs!' she called to Priscilla. And Priscilla did, taking care to make them soft yet crispy and to serve them so they didn't slide off the plate into the government man's lap.

'What is it, Aunty?' she said, anxious, when the man was gone. Aunty sat brooding at the table in front of the now empty dishes.

'New regulations, child,' she said, in English.

Priscilla's heart swelled into her mouth and her belly dropped and went cold. Aunty only ever called her *child* when she wanted to be gentle, when there was terrible or difficult news to tell, such as when Achu had been hit by a bus and killed.

The new regulations were that the boys must be housed in a separate building if they were to stay. Aunty had no money for a separate building, she said. The boys, who she was as attached to now as the girls, would have to go.

It took a year, and after that, somehow, Aunty seemed to lose heart in everything. She said she was getting old, she couldn't do this any more.

Letters were written, relatives came from distant places to talk to Aunty. In the end homes and jobs and one or two college places were found for the girls, husbands for the two oldest ones.

By the time Priscilla was eighteen, or possibly nineteen – it was hard to know for sure; she'd been such a tiny, toothless thing when she was found that no one, not even Aunty, knew exactly how old she was – she was the only girl left, and one Sunday Aunty waylaid the Padre after church and asked him if he could take her.

He was on his own now, the Padre, and everyone knew he wasn't looking after himself properly, that he existed on fryums and tea, up there in the presbytery without his wife and his daughter and with only the occasional foreign missionary and the dog, Ooly, for company, and everyone knew what a mournful and undemonstrative creature she was. His brothers in Chennai never visited. Priscilla would be a breath of fresh air around the place, said Aunty. She was young and cheerful, she could cook and she could clean and she could go shopping.

When the Padre said he would think about it, the old woman put her hand on his sleeve.

'Andrew,' she said. 'Please. She has no one.'

31

Byrd was alone in the presbytery drawing room when he noticed the sewing machine.

His second reading lesson with Priscilla was over and he was gathering his books, ready to go back to his bungalow. Priscilla was in the kitchen and the Padre was out in the hall, making a phone call.

A heavy cloth covering the big machine had slipped to the floor, exposing it where it stood, next to the window. It looked very old and was equipped with a large, rusty foot treadle. Byrd approached it. Wheeler & Wilson, it said in gold letters along the top. He bent down, curious to see if he could figure out how the treadle mechanism worked.

'You are an expert, Mr Byrd?'

The Padre had appeared with his usual suddenness and absence of announcement and was standing now, at Byrd's shoulder.

'Oh no, not at all,' said Byrd, but he did, he said, know how to sew.

By now Priscilla had appeared in the doorway too. Byrd and the Padre were squatting in front of the big machine, the Padre watching while Hilary Byrd pushed down with his hand on the iron lattice-work of the foot treadle.

Perhaps, said the Padre, glancing from Hilary Byrd to Priscilla and back again to Byrd's bent and folded form, if it was not too much trouble, and Mr Byrd could spare the time, he might teach Priscilla, on top of the reading and the writing, a little of what he knew about sewing?

Byrd hesitated.

The machine looked as ancient as an old spinning wheel. He'd never heard of Wheeler & Wilson and he'd never used a treadle before. His mother had owned an electrified Singer and his aunt a Bernina; he and Wyn had learned to use both, but neither the Singer nor the Bernina was anything like this. Here in the hills, he'd watched the tailors in their little cubicles at the market, working the treadles with their bare feet, looking as if they were paddling lightly on top of a swiftly moving river and although it looked easy, Byrd suspected it wasn't. He noticed that the large rubber band that ran around the little wheel at the top of the Padre's machine and the big wheel at the bottom was held together with a staple.

He would have to practise, he said.

The Padre clapped his hands. 'Come, Mr Byrd, let us push it out into the room.'

Very softly, as the two men bent over the machine and pushed, the Padre whispered, 'I am giving the machine to Priscilla, for when she is married. It will be a good thing for her, to know how to make things.'

If Mr Hilary Byrd would accept it, he would give him some money so that in the morning he could buy what he needed at the draper's in the market, and Byrd, who never liked spending his own money and was always worried about running out of it, nodded. He would buy some cloth, he said, and needles and pins and thread and some chalk. A decent pair of dressmaking scissors and, if possible, some pinking shears.

'Good, Mr Byrd. Very good!'

A faraway look had come into the Padre's eyes, which were gazing now, out of the window across the garden, as if he could see, snaking in through the gateless opening from the road and along the driveway to the front door, a procession of respectable and gainfully employed young men, all of them wanting to marry Priscilla.

Priscilla laughed and so did the Padre – the Padre laughed till he cried – when Byrd set the treadle going for the first time and the old machine bounded across the rug like a kangaroo.

'Don't laugh!' said Byrd, laughing himself. 'I've never used one of these things before!'

He thought of the tailors at the market, working their metal foot-plates as if they were walking on water.

'Hold on,' he said, hauling the machine back in front of his chair. 'There's a knack. I just need to get the hang of it.'

Which, in due course, he did, and then he showed Priscilla how to get the hang of it too, and by the end of their first lesson he'd shown her how to make a pattern out of newspaper and pin the pieces on the fabric for a tunic – a kurti, Priscilla called it – and a pair of trousers; how to mark up the fabric with a flat piece of pink chalk and how to place the tailor's tacks; how to tease the folded cloth apart and snip the tacks so each piece retained the necessary threads which would show her, later, how to connect everything together.

It embarrassed him to lay the paper pieces on the folded cloth that represented Priscilla's two legs, one longer than the other, but Priscilla did not seem to mind. She looked bright and interested and wanted to do everything herself. 'Show me, Uncle, show me,' she kept saying. 'Let me, let me.'

It touched him that she called him *Uncle*. He was nobody's uncle, only someone's brother. It seemed a nice way for her to address him.

He had never seen her hands up close before. He'd expected a scar or some nubbly tissue, something vestigial perhaps, but there was nothing, they were perfectly smooth, like something carved and polished, like marble, a flat plane, nothing at all where her thumbs should be, as if, rather than forgetting them, nature had decided to experiment with leaving them out. The chalk, the needle, the pins, the cutting-out scissors, the heavy pinking shears – she gripped them all between the second and third fingers of her left hand. Only the pinking shears seemed, after ploughing for a long time around the edge of the newspaper pattern through the folded cloth, to wear her out.

'Priscilla, can I –' but she took no notice of him, carried on crunching through the patterned cloth, her front teeth locked into the pink furrow of her bottom lip, dark eyes fixed on where she was heading, as if her life depended on it.

'Perfect,' said Byrd quietly. Tomorrow he would show her how to do the seams and set in the sleeves of the tunic. If there was time, they would assemble the trousers too, and she could learn how to make a waistband and thread a piece of elastic through it on the end of a safety pin.

'Thank you, Uncle. Thank you.'

32

She'd never lost it, that feeling of being safest when she was wrapped up.

So there will be some sort of cloak or dupatta, for sure, to go with the trousers and the kurti and anything else Mr Hilary Byrd can show her how to make.

With a cloak or dupatta, she will feel capable and brave and ready.

But for now, there was the homework he gave her – story after story copied out in the red exercise book, care taken to keep her loping letters inside the graph-paper squares. The Padre watching them from his chair in the corner, looking up from time to time and resting his eyes on her, kindly but worried also, constantly – she saw it in his old eyes – about what will happen to her when he's gone; thinking all the time about his search for a boy.

She'd noticed that he'd added a little more gold to the things in the metal trunk.

Also, yesterday, he told her that the big Wheeler & Wilson sewing machine would be hers once she was married. Most things in the presbytery belonged to the church and he was not at liberty to give them away, but the Wheeler & Wilson sewing machine had belonged to his wife so he could give her that. And meanwhile God had sent them Mr Hilary Byrd from Petts Wood UK, who knew how to sew and was also, conveniently, a librarian, and happy with books and could help her with her English while the Padre was busy.

All of it, said the Padre – the sewing machine, the learning – would be sure to help.

'Praise the Lord!' he was fond of saying spontaneously at intervals during the day, 'for bringing us Mr Hilary Byrd!'

'Yes, Uncle,' said Priscilla.

The books Mr Byrd brought to the presbytery to teach her included the same horrible old books from the UK that Aunty had had.

The same silly boring titles, the same difficult words looming in a dreadful way on the page opposite bright pictures of kittens and armies of men and balls of wool and golden coaches and beanstalks. The same horrible thing about every book: every single one exactly 56 pages long. *Florence Nightingale* and *The Story of Ships*, *Puss in Boots* and *The Weather* and *Sly Fox* and *The Night Sky* and *The Magic Porridge Pot* and *Things to Make* (stupid stilts of string and tin cans, a snake made of cotton reels painted green with yellow spots) – they all had exactly the same number of pages. She hated that; it made her feel trapped somehow, as if there were certain things in the world you could never change and certain pointless rules that could never, ever be broken.

Still, she was trying her best now, with Mr Byrd.

She gripped the cardboard covers between her eight strong fingers and concentrated. She moved slowly forward from word to word; sometimes she hung on one for ages, trying to unpick the letters and remember in exactly which particular way their pronunciation did not resemble their appearance. *Bough. Bow. Pour. Poor.* It did not help when Uncle told her that a lot of English grammar was the result of Viking people speaking it very badly – that they were the reason the verbs were so simple. It did not help being told that something was easy when it wasn't. Sometimes she wanted to smack him on the arm for trying to help her when she was still in the middle of trying to puzzle things out. 'Buh –' he'd start saying, leaning over her like a big stooping plant. 'Shh, no, Uncle,' she'd said tonight, and she must have sounded cross because he'd blushed and gone very quiet, and she'd been sorry afterwards because she felt that she had hurt him a little, with the harshness of her *shh*.

She liked him, in spite of the horrible books. He was patient and never shouted, and more than once, in the last few weeks, when the Padre was out of the room on the telephone, or when he'd gone to fetch some document or piece of paper from upstairs, she'd thought perhaps she could tell him everything, and had actually begun:

'Uncle –?'

'Yes, Priscilla?'

He'd looked at her with his pale, blinking eyes and she'd felt she was going to speak but then she'd lost her nerve, and asked some question instead about the seam allowance and how they were going to get the elastic through the space they'd made for it at the top of the trousers; how you actually did that with a safety pin.

She'd been thinking a lot lately about the day Aunty had brought her to the presbytery for the first time to ask the Padre if he would give her a home.

She remembered Aunty telling him (though Priscilla was sure he must know the story already) of how Aunty had found her hidden in the bushes by the lake shore, and how Priscilla had seemed to be about seven years old, though it was hard to tell, because she was so small and malnourished and had no teeth.

She remembered Aunty exclaiming to the Padre, 'Oh, Padre, I prayed so hard for those teeth!' and she remembered how true that was – how Aunty had cried out, when the first rough edge of a front tooth had emerged, 'Praise the Lord!' and how after that Aunty had kept on praying and crying out, 'Praise the Lord!' each time another tooth came through, until eventually, over the course of a year, all of Priscilla's teeth had followed. Which was a relief, it was true – Priscilla had become sure that she'd have to go through her whole life without any teeth at all. But it didn't mean she was going to thank God for them. Her short right leg and her absence of thumbs had long ago convinced her that if there was a God, he was not a kind one, and he did not love her.

Still, the Padre had been kind. He'd given her a home, and for his sake, she pretended to love God.

It was one of the foreign volunteers at Aunty's who'd left behind the CD.

She'd found it under one of the bunkbeds when she was cleaning out the volunteers' dormitory after they left and before the new ones arrived. The clear plastic case was cracked; from a picture on the paper beneath, a dark-haired woman in a white scarf and a fringed shirt looked out, smiling. She'd slipped it under her tunic and crept into Aunty's office downstairs, which was not allowed, and put the CD into the player only the foreign volunteers had permission to use, and – oh!

A sweet, deep voice that took her breath away and made her think she hadn't been alive till now.

From the market, having no money to buy one, she stole another CD with the same dark-haired woman in the picture beneath the plastic cover – Priscilla would have recognised her anywhere. This time wearing a studded waistcoat and boots and a skirt and a white hat like a cowboy's. The same shape to the biggest two words on the front which Priscilla thought must certainly signify a name. A *P* at the beginning – the sound you made in English by pressing your lips together and letting go of a small explosion. The other letters she wasn't sure about, but the *P* she recognised.

She slipped the case inside the loose sleeve of her tunic and hurried away as fast as her two uneven legs would carry her and the next chance she got she played it in Aunty's office when Aunty was out and the younger children were at school and the new foreign volunteers were sleeping, and from out of the speakers it was the same deep, sweet voice that came, singing words which were often indecipherable but seemed nevertheless to Priscilla to contain all the feelings she'd ever known. In every line she heard pain, and longing and a slow, crooning desire.

Little by little she learned to sing the words, listening over and over to the songs, though still without fully understanding their meaning. In time, she was able to identify the titles of the lyrics written on the folded paper under the clear plastic cover of the CD: *Walkin' After Midnight. There He Goes. Crazy.*

She began paying attention during the hour Aunty set aside

each week to help her with her English. Reading with Aunty was still a torture; she still hated staring at the impossible shapes on the page, willing them to open themselves up and tell her what they were, Aunty trying to sound patient but sounding mean and cross. 'Come on now, girl. This word you know. This word we had last week. Try, girl.' And she did try, and soon she discovered that the name of the dark-haired woman was Patsy Cline. Patsy, the word beginning with *P.* At the market she found Reba McEntire and Bonnie Raitt. Garth Brooks and Johnny Cash and Kris Kristofferson.

And always the thin young man with the shiny hair and the big moustache and the white cowboy hat hanging around the same stall, picking through the same CDs that she was.

33

And then the Padre discovered that Hilary Byrd not only knew how to sew, he could bake too.

'I was brought up like Henry VIII,' exclaimed Byrd ebulliently one day – very jolly and relaxed now after a week of reading lessons and sewing classes – 'by women. Only instead of jousting and playing the lute and writing poetry, I learned to make cakes and sew.'

When Priscilla had gone to bed, the Padre asked, in a gently inquiring voice – a little anxiously, perhaps, as if he thought he might be pushing his luck, 'Baking also then, Mr Byrd, sir?'

Dear Wyn, Byrd wrote.

So now we are baking and sewing as well as reading and writing!

The reading and the writing, he told her, were going extremely well. Priscilla was very diligent and seemed to have a fairly quick mind, though he thought they would have to get a long way beyond *The Frog Prince* if he were to help make up for her disadvantages, but so far, so good.

Meanwhile I've taught her how to make a paper pattern; how to do tailor's tacks, how to make darts and do an ordinary seam and a French seam, how to interface a yoke and do pleats and buttonholes and put in a zip and blind-stitch a hem and thread *a piece of elastic through a waistband with a safety pin. We've made a pair of trousers and a tunic. We have also made shortbread and a Victoria sponge and chocolate brownies and this evening we are making scones. 'Praise the Lord!' shouts the Padre, clapping his hands whenever Priscilla finishes a seam or a buttonhole or takes a cake out of the presbytery's funny little oven. Every day he looks happier and more hopeful, and I – oh, Wyn, I am feeling <u>well</u>. I really am. Better than I've felt in ages.*

It was true. He felt, for once, that he was in exactly the right place at exactly the right time. For longer than he could remember, he had felt, at the library, like a stranger in a foreign land, surrounded by alien goings-on.

In Modern Stores, he bought a packet of Be-Ro self-raising flour and butter and a box of Tate & Lyle caster sugar, a bag of milk, sultanas, a jar of Hartley's strawberry jam, and an egg.

In the presbytery kitchen he showed Priscilla and the Padre how to rub the butter into the flour, then sprinkle in the dried fruit and sugar and stir in the milk and the beaten egg and how to gather it up into a ball and roll it out onto the floured surface of the table; how not to knead it and slap it about too much but keep it thick and cool so it would rise quickly in the heat of the small, round electric oven that sat on top of the counter and was plugged into the wall. Together they peered over the clear lid of the oven until Priscilla jumped up and down – lightly on her good left foot, heavily with a dull, muted thump on the big boot of her right. 'Scones are coming up, Uncle!' she called out, looking at Byrd as if she hadn't believed they would rise as he'd promised they would, and now that they had, she considered it a piece of magic for which he was personally responsible.

When the scones were cool, Priscilla arranged them on a round white plate and Byrd spooned strawberry jam into a small yellow bowl, and in the shabby dining room of the old presbytery, they ate them, and when there was nothing left on the white plate but a few crumbs, the Padre said, 'Thank you, Mr Byrd, we thank you!' and when Priscilla had taken the empty plate back into the kitchen he winked, and whispered, 'I think Priscilla's husband will have to be a thin man.'

34

Jamshed sat with the graph-paper exercise book in his lap.

Today coming back from his outing on the lake Mr Byrd is telling a story about making cakes with the Padre and the Padre's crippled orphan girl called Priscilla.

Ten days in a row now, Mr Byrd had been sprightly and excited and full of cheer. Ten days in a row now he had not mentioned his library once, nor his Chinese lessons nor his Russian ones. He had not talked about his feelings of hopelessness or how gloomy and sad his home made him feel or how paralysed he was sometimes by the thought of everything he didn't know. He had not repeated what he'd said about being born into darkness.

   Yesterday, he'd taken the train down to Coonoor to visit the tea plantation, and had come back chattering about everything he'd learned there – spouting all kinds of things about tea as if he was telling Jamshed things Jamshed didn't already know. What a fine plant the tea plant was! 'Did you know, Jamshed, that if you prune it every six to seven years, it will go on producing fresh leaves for a century? Did you know that on a medium-sized plantation, by the time you've finished picking the last leaf on the last bush, it's time to go back to the first bush and start all over again – there will already be new leaves coming?'

Later, at the lake, he'd hired a boat, and from inside his auto, Jamshed had watched him rowing himself out into the middle of the water – the sun shining on him, not a single drop of rain falling on his shoulders or his head, looking very glad to be here in these foreign hills, away from the raucous mothers and toddlers and Margaret the librarian – away from his useless doctor and the familiar carpets of his boyhood home and the girl in the flowery dress who had spoken to him so unkindly.

Then, to Jamshed's very great surprise, he'd done something he'd never done before: he invited Jamshed to come out with him in the boat.

Jamshed had hesitated – aware, suddenly, that he wanted more than anything to sit in a rowing boat opposite Mr Byrd in the middle of the lake. The problem was, he was terrified of the water – Jamshed could no more swim than he could fly, and the small flat boats tied to the landing looked as flimsy as a pile of leaves. 'Come on, Jamshed! Come with me!' Mr Byrd had called out to him. But Jamshed could only dither and sit, wavering, half in and half out of his auto, black flip-flop foot in the cab and red plastic clog foot on the lake shore, thinking yes-no-yes-no-yes. Eventually calling back, 'No thank you, sir! I am staying here!'

He was happy though. Happy that Mr Byrd had asked him. In all the weeks that he'd been driving him around the town, he'd always had the feeling that it hardly mattered to Mr Byrd if he was there at all – that he could have replaced himself with a lump of wood, or a potato, and Mr Byrd would not have noticed. He would have gone on talking or sitting there in one of his long silences and it would have made no difference to him at all if Jamshed was in the cab or if he wasn't.

The old man had been lost in his own thoughts when Mr Byrd appeared later at his shoulder, flushed from his outing on the water, smiling, and saying he would like to go now, please, to the chocolate shop.

35

What happened came to pass with such swiftness and force it left Byrd reeling, winded.

Cool, misty days, grey and mild, followed one after another.

Byrd touched his cheek and wondered if it was broken. There'd been a crack like a hard-skinned fruit splitting when he landed at the bottom of the market steps; then nothing, only a drip-drip-drip he remembered hoping was the rain and not the pitter-patter of his own blood. 'Hurting you, Uncle?'

Priscilla was looking at him. She'd stopped reading.

He was a little startled. 'Hurting me? Oh no, not really. Not too much anyway, Priscilla. It looks a lot worse than it is.'

Which was, he thought, even if it *was* broken, probably true; if it was broken, all he had to do was wait for it to mend itself. Meanwhile beyond the dull ache, which was worse in the evenings than it was in the mornings, he almost forgot about his injury for long periods during the day. But it still *looked* awful. Although the thundery blue-black had long since faded, his face still, after all these weeks, resembled a terrible relief map of contused green and yellow and, in some places, brown.

'I look a bit like the Lake District,' he said, laughing gently at his own joke.

Priscilla's own face was scrunched up in what seemed to him like sympathetic but sceptical amazement. Her eyes travelled over his chin and his forehead and his cheeks, between his severely bloodshot left eye and his reasonably clear right one, as if she didn't believe he was telling the truth and thought he must really be in considerable pain.

He found himself looking directly into her eyes for the first time. They were very dark, and he couldn't see his own reflection in them. She held his gaze steadily, confidently, and in the end, he was forced to look away.

Then the day came when he locked himself out of his bungalow.

He knew he'd done it as soon as he closed the door; he knew that the key was not in his jacket pocket. He didn't even need to pat the pocket to know it wasn't here, he could feel its absence, and when he looked in through the window he could see it on the shelf above his desk. He walked all the way round the outside of the bungalow and tried all the windows but they were all closed on the inside. Then he saw Priscilla at the back door of the presbytery.

'Priscilla!'

His voice was loud in the still garden. Through the glass of the drawing room he saw the Padre look up from his desk.

Priscilla inspected the door, all the windows. 'There is the key, Uncle,' she said, pointing to the key inside on the shelf.

They both pressed their faces to the window, cupping their hands around their faces.

'Yes,' said Byrd. 'I know. Does the Padre have another one by any chance? A spare?'

But Priscilla was already stumping off towards the garage and returning with one of the short-handled tools with a curved blade Byrd had seen the women in the field beside the shortcut using.

'Wait here, Uncle,' said Priscilla.

And then she was prising open one of the windows at the front of his bungalow and clambering over the sill and disappearing inside until suddenly she was in front of him, opening his own front door, smiling triumphantly and holding out the rescued key.

'Thank you, Priscilla.'

'Yes, Uncle.'

He put the key in the pocket of his trousers.

'Thank you,' he said again, and again she said, 'Yes, Uncle,' but this time she added that, really, he should keep his windows open a little always, to let some air blow in. Weren't his things damp, with all the windows closed like that?

Yes, they were, a little, said Byrd.

His clothes felt slightly damp when he put them on in the morning, and the covers of the paperback books he'd brought with him from England were curled like pea-shooters. There was even, he'd noticed, in his bathroom, a small, pale, mushroomy thing growing in the corner of the window frame.

Priscilla was nodding and laughing a little. 'Because you keep the windows closed, Uncle. Open them and everything will not be so damp.'

Byrd had thought of doing this, but it had worried him, the idea of leaving his bungalow unsecured and open to intruders – some thief from the town getting in and stealing his money and his passport, or the Padre's smelly dog hopping up onto the window ledge and breaching his defences at last. He'd been worried that he might come back one afternoon and find

Ooly lying on the rug in front of his fire, or worse, in his bed. He confessed this last part now, to Priscilla. 'I think I'm a little afraid of her.' Priscilla laughed again.

'Oh, Uncle! She is only lazy and a little bit naughty. She will not hurt you.'

They were standing together now in the verandah-like room at the front, looking down at the dog in her sink. On the wire washing line a necklace of raindrops hung suspended from the last shower and twinkled in the sunshine. 'Look at her, Uncle. How can you be afraid of her?'

Byrd looked and it was true – Ooly did not seem like anything to be frightened of. She seemed to be sleeping and breathing peacefully. Only her triangular ears moved, flicking and twitching irregularly, as if she were dreaming and experiencing small, surprising moments of drama and excitement.

Well, said Byrd, maybe he'd risk leaving his windows open, just a little bit, from now on.

When Priscilla was gone, he went around his bungalow, unlatching them all. Somehow her suggesting it made it seem practical, usual, the 'done thing'. In fact, it was a pleasurable thought, the chill air blowing up the valley and in through his partly open windows, riffling the pages of his books, causing his clothes to sway on their hangers, airing the damp, drooping towel in his bathroom. It felt like a sort of cleansing, an opening of his arms to the fresh, fresh sky.

'I thought we could make meringues,' he said.

It was what he decided as soon as he woke up: that instead

of going into town he would go over to the presbytery with half a dozen eggs, some caster sugar and some vinegar.

And they had a lively time, the three of them in the kitchen, Hilary Byrd, Priscilla and the Padre, just as they had with the scones, and before that, with the shortbread and the chocolate brownies and the Victoria sponge – Priscilla disappointed at first when Byrd said they needed a whisk and a whisk was something they didn't have, but relieved when he said it was all right, a fork would do. Priscilla wide-eyed and delighted when the transformation of the egg-whites began; the Padre getting so carried away he was in danger of over-beating them and Byrd had to confiscate his fork.

It was a messy business. At the end of it even Byrd's socks were spattered with the mixture.

Back in his bungalow, he boiled a pan of water and then another one, undressed, and put everything he was wearing to soak in hot water in the tall pink bucket in his bathroom. While he was at it, he threw in a few more items of dirty laundry that were in his bedroom and in need of washing. Dark clouds of dirt billowed out into the clean, soapy water beneath his hands. Wearing only his underwear, he tipped the clothes out onto the tiled floor of the bungalow's bathroom and boiled more water; refilled the big pink bucket. Rinsed everything with cold water from the tap, and repeated. Squeezed out as much water as he could, then put on clean socks and a fresh shirt and a pair of trousers and hauled everything out to the metal line between his bungalow and the boiler house.

'No, Uncle!'

Priscilla was in the kitchen doorway at the back of the presbytery, pointing at the sky. 'Rain is coming!'

Byrd stood. He held one of his washed shirts by the shoulders against the line. He had two coloured plastic pegs in his mouth, ready to pin them on. He tipped his head up to the sky, where here and there a few pale, misty clouds drifted in an expanse of white. Nothing about the clouds seemed to him to be in any way threatening. The sky looked, in fact, much clearer than usual. He took the pegs out of his mouth.

'How can you tell?'

'Clouds, Uncle.'

'But there are always clouds, Priscilla. How can you tell when it's actually going to rain? How do you do that?'

Priscilla lifted her shoulders and said it was practice. You just looked at them and watched and saw what happened and after a while you came to know which way things would go, whether the rain would come or whether it wouldn't.

'I see,' said Byrd, working his way along the line, pulling off the pegs he'd already pinned on and gathering them in his fist, draping his wet clothing over his shoulder. But he didn't see. Cloudy or clear, it was no indication that there might be showers later. He went on to the end of the line until all of his wet, washed clothes hung over both of his arms and his hands were full of pegs. Priscilla pointed to the far end of the line and he saw that one black sock remained. He snatched it off with his teeth and when he looked back at Priscilla she was laughing, covering her mouth with one of her thumbless hands.

After that he didn't see her again until evening, when he was crossing the garden to the presbytery with the book of Andersen fairy stories under his arm, ready for their evening lesson, and she emerged, suddenly, from the trees.

She gave a small cry, and covered her mouth, like before, with her hand.

'Oh, Uncle, I didn't see you there!' she said, in a flustered whisper, and it amazed him, what he felt. It took his breath away, how much it pained him, to hear her call him *Uncle*.

36

He couldn't explain it. He hardly knew her.

Every day now, before he went into town, he stood at his window, looking out across the garden, waiting for her to appear. When she didn't come, he wished she would.

There were times when he walked out along the driveway and thought he could hear the rapid, uneven music of her distinctive walk just behind him, but when he turned there was nothing, and he was aware that the sound of her had been conjured, not by the shuffle of the leafy pom-poms of the eucalyptus trees in the wind, but by his own hope.

They'd never really had a proper conversation. The only times he'd been alone with her was the day she'd told him it was going to rain, and the day she helped him break into his bungalow. There were the hours he spent listening to her read, and helping her with her spelling; there was the sewing they did together, and the baking, but the Padre, on all these occasions, was always present, including the time she'd asked him if his face hurt. It was rare, too, for them to talk about anything other than the task in hand. In the three and a half weeks since he'd started teaching her, they'd swapped only the most meagre details of their different lives, and always within earshot of the Padre. Once, Byrd had asked her where she'd lived before she came to the presbytery, and she told him she'd lived with twenty-seven other children with someone she called Aunty. She'd told him about Aunty's ambitions for their education. About the foreign volunteers from Europe and Scandinavia and North America who came and stayed for three months and then vanished and you never heard from them again. He, in turn, told her that he had worked for most of his life in a library but didn't any more. He told her that before he arrived here in the hills, he'd been to Chennai and Trichy and Thanjavur. To Tranquebar to visit the old Danish fort; to Pondicherry to see the houses the French had left behind. He told her he'd wanted to go to Delhi, and to Agra to see the Taj Mahal. He'd always wanted to see the Taj Mahal, he said. It looked so beautiful in all the pictures. The glittering white, the long stretch of water in front like a pea-green carpet. But the heat had defeated him, he told her, and he'd come here instead.

The only moment they'd shared which had felt in any way intimate or private was yesterday when, out of the blue, she'd passed him a tiny folded piece of paper.

The Padre had just stepped out of the room to answer the phone.

'Uncle,' she whispered. 'Please. Read this.'

Byrd's heart had begun to beat crazily. He'd looked at her and then at the paper. What was he hoping for? He couldn't say. The paper was folded into four. He opened it.

Arkansas, he read.

Just that, in Priscilla's large, round handwriting. She was looking up at him.

'It says Arkansas,' he whispered, whispering because she had whispered.

'Arkansas,' she repeated softly, earnestly, taking the scrap of paper from him and folding her fingers around it. 'Thank you, Uncle.'

And then the Padre was in the room again, settling himself into his chair in the corner with his glasses on his nose and his yellow pad on his lap.

Byrd looked out now, over the empty garden.

The Dorothy Perkins rose – abundant and full and very tall against the wall of the presbytery, had bloomed for a second time. In the herbaceous borders dahlias were in flower, bronze and purple and white.

What was it that he felt?

Was it that she made him feel useful? Was it that she made him feel needed, necessary?

Or was it pity? Was it pity that made him imagine the two of them walking in through the door of his bungalow, and laughing at the way Ooly would be trying to worm her way in as well? Was it pity that made him imagine himself shouting, 'Out, Ooly! You dreadful hound. Be gone! Leave us alone!' Was it pity that made him imagine Priscilla saying, 'Poor Ooly, I think she's jealous.' Was it pity that made him stand here, waiting for her to appear? Was it pity that made him imagine her calling him Hilary?

He didn't think so. What he knew for certain was that she'd become important to him somehow. He didn't know how but she had. One thing had led to another, and he had not expected any of it.

Through the window he could see the dog, lying in her sink, gazing up at him. With her black nose resting on its favourite place on the lip of the sink, and her dark eyes lifted to his window, she looked more miserable than ever, as if she understood that everything had changed. That it was all different now, and it made her unspeakably sad.

37

What Byrd did, was to try and carry on, as far as possible, as before, sticking to his daily routine: leaving his bungalow in the mornings to meet Jamshed at the bottom of the steps, and doing the rounds of his favourite places in the town.

He went to the market and the chocolate shop and strolled in the Botanical Gardens and along the edge of the lake. Sometimes he rented a rowing boat.

In the afternoons he went to the library and sat in his usual chair opposite the buffalo's head and tried to read. When he couldn't, he walked out of the library and through the wooded grounds around it to the low wall at its outer edge, and from there up the hill. On these occasions he told Jamshed not to wait; he would walk home, he needed the exercise. Sometimes he cut through St Peter's churchyard and took the path between the collapsing gravestones. As he walked he scanned the inscriptions – the names and dates of the British who'd come here and made the place their own: the soldiers and the doctors, the officials and their wives and sometimes their children and their babies; the ones who'd never left, who were planted here in the earth.

From the perimeter he could see right across the town – the partially roofed warren of the market in the middle; to the west the almost black surface of the lake, to the east the green interlude of the Botanical Gardens. He could see the old racecourse and the red tiles of the Savoy, and the white building in the jewellery district where the Zoroastrians went to pray and talk and do whatever it was Zoroastrians did. He could see the spires of St Mary's Catholic church and St Peter's Protestant church and the delicate towers of the two mosques; the fairy-cake colours of the two largest Hindu temples.

Down on the plains he'd wandered through temples with courtyards the size of football fields, past galleries of brightly clothed and garlanded gods, while families picnicked and slept in the cool shade between pillars, and monks walked in their sunshine-coloured robes. On the way into the temples, he'd been anxious about having to give up his shoes, certain that such places would be full of people who would surely prefer his to their own. He could no longer remember the names of most of the gods, nor their special powers, though he thought Vishnu might be the blue one, and that Ganesh was the elephant one, and had something to do with new beginnings and the removal of obstacles. He had no clue as to the meaning of the painted marks so many of the people wore on their foreheads, which were the same here, as far as he could tell, as they were in the cities of the plains. Sometimes they were dots and sometimes they were lines, sometimes they were red and sometimes they were white, and other times they were black and reminded him of the ashy smudges you saw on foreheads at home to mark the beginning of Lent, but whether they signified repentance or devotion or grief or something else entirely, he had no idea.

He turned away from the panorama of the town and carried on up the hill, leaving the churchyard behind, and all the time he was preoccupied and looking forward anxiously to the evening, when he would see Priscilla. Nothing had changed about the way things proceeded. To all outward appearances they were exactly the same as before: if they were baking in the kitchen, the Padre generally participated; if not, and they were sewing or reading in the drawing room, the old clergyman mostly sat quietly in the corner with his head bent over his yellow pad. Only now, a single thought was going round and round in Byrd's head.

What does she think of me?

38

It was the Padre's idea that they should play Scrabble.

His daughter's set lay on top of the ancient piano and one evening when Byrd arrived with his books, the old clergyman said, why didn't he teach Priscilla to play? It would be a change from the reading and the writing and it would be good for her spelling. He would sit in the corner and get on with his work. 'I will be quiet as a mouse,' he said, beaming.

So Byrd and Priscilla played Scrabble. Byrd set up the board and they picked their tiles and Byrd asked Priscilla, 'What's your Scrabble name going to be?'

'Scrabble name, Uncle?'

'Yes.' When he played with his sister, said Byrd, they always chose a special name to play under.

'What sort of name?'

'Oh, you know, anything. A *nom de guerre*. Something, you know, a bit silly. Something ironic or amusing.' He was Mah-Jongg sometimes, for example, which was the name of a famous lemur which had once lived in a palace near his home, and his sister was quite often Margaret, because if Wyn was Margaret then he tried harder to beat her and it was very satisfying when he did. He could explain it, he said, but it was a long story.

'So anyway, tonight, I could be, say,' – he searched his imagination and his memory for a name and thought of the soldiers' gravestones in St Peter's cemetery – 'Major Percy Lushington. And you' – he searched again and thought of the sticker which was on one of the mirrors at the draper's stall in the market advertising Surinder shawls – 'can be Surinder Shawl.'

Priscilla laughed. 'OK, Uncle.'

Silently they studied their tiles.

'You have many sisters, Uncle?'

'No, Priscilla. Just one.'

'Brothers?'

'No.'

'Parents?'

'Not any more.'

'Married, Uncle?'

'No.'

Byrd felt himself redden. The directness of her question both surprised and elated him. It felt like the first piece of concrete encouragement she'd given him and he took hold of it with both hands. He would love to kiss her now, and for the first time he let himself imagine what that might be like. He had no experience. None. There'd never been anything, ever. It was not what he'd expected but it was the way things had gone. Once, at university, he'd stumbled into the wrong room and in the half-dark had witnessed skin and movement and an urgent, feral heat before backing out like a courtier, falling over his own feet, wanting simultaneously to vanish and stay where he was. Later – briefly and a long time ago now – there'd been Elaine. Except there hadn't, not really. For a while she'd come often to the library on a Saturday, and eventually he'd been aware that she sought him out. Always a question about a particular book she couldn't find, or to ask him if he could order one for her from another library. Sometimes she came to him with a book recommendation of her own – something she'd read and thought he might enjoy, which was how they'd come to go to the cinema together. *Dances with Wolves*, Elaine had said, was a very good book which had now been turned into a film, and although he did not believe what she said about it being a good book, he had gone with her and in the darkness he could tell that she was stirred by one of the scenes, the one where the daughter of the Medicine Man was in the tent with the man who had once been a soldier in the Civil War. He'd felt it in the position of her body next to his, the way she was holding herself, and when they'd come outside she'd stood in front of him and rested her head on his shoulder and he knew this was his cue to act but he'd done nothing. His heart was beating quickly but he'd been certain that if he acted he would disgrace himself somehow. He'd wished she would do something more than just lean against him with her head – that she would lead so he could follow, but she hadn't, and after a few moments she'd stepped away from him. He knew he'd embarrassed her, and he told her he was sorry, and then she was gone, and he was not surprised when she didn't come again to the library.

He'd grown used to it, that side of things not being part of his life. He'd ceased long ago to expect it and gradually, over the years, had become more and more afraid of it. He and Wyn never talked about it. She'd never taken on the role of inquisitor and he understood that this was out of kindness. She'd given him the slippers for Miss Yu – had bought them with her Harrods discount and brought them home and wrapped them up so he could take them to his Chinese lesson with his mince pies. But she hadn't inquired about his feelings, about whether anything like that had become mixed up in it all, with his learning of this new language. Looking back, he wasn't sure himself.

What would Priscilla do if he kissed her now? If he just – but it was impossible of course, with the Padre there. With the Padre there, kissing her would break all the rules. He didn't know what the rules were but he was sure that kissing her now would break them.

He played carefully, using only his low-scoring letters and the Padre was delighted when Priscilla showed him the score: Major Percy Lushington 102. Surinder Shawl 116.

In the weeks that followed, they played Scrabble three more times and made their way through Andersen's fairy tales and the remaining Ladybird books, plus some new ones by the Brothers Grimm; Priscilla reading, Byrd listening and gently correcting her pronunciation; the Padre looking up from time to time from his work; Byrd's concentration drifting.

Listening to Priscilla reading *Puss in Boots,* he took in nothing of the story. He didn't stop her to tell her she was putting the emphasis in the wrong place; he didn't stop her to ask if she understood what she was reading.

Did she talk about him ever, to the Padre?

And what did the Padre think of him, actually? Byrd had no idea, not really, and he was certain it mattered, what the Padre thought. The old clergyman was always friendly, and very effusive in his thanks for the teaching and the sewing and the baking, but beyond that, it was impossible to know what his opinion was. How could you ever tell what another person thought of you? In the whole place, only the dog, Ooly, seemed to wear her heart on her sleeve, her scraggy forepaw. Her big, sad eyes full of longing and despair.

In the Botanical Gardens he strolled along the winding gravel paths, forcing himself to concentrate on the explanatory placards that were stuck into the ground beside the trees and shrubs. He paused in front of the Australian conifers and the Spanish chestnuts; the enormous poplar with its unexpectedly rough and furrowed trunk; the four delicate acers; the soapnut tree with its clusters of golden pods.

It was raining again, and chilly, the monsoon being nothing like he'd expected. He'd imagined torrents and floods and mudslides, but instead the days were a mix of patchy sun and intermittent showers he still found impossible to predict.

He bent down so that he was closer to the small metal placard speared into the ground near his feet.

The eucalyptus, he read, *is not a native species.*

Byrd almost exclaimed aloud. The eucalyptus – not a native species!

There was nothing in the whole of the town, nor on the slopes of the hills around it, that was so completely ubiquitous, so absolutely all-over-everywhere, as the eucalyptus tree. With their bundles of untidy silver-green leaves and pale, moulting trunks, they grew like weeds everywhere he looked.

He read on.

The seeds of the eucalyptus tree were brought here in the

nineteenth century from Tasmania by the soldiers of the Madras
regiment of the British Indian army.

'Well how about that,' said Byrd quietly.

Back in the cab of Jamshed's auto, he told the old driver about the trees and how it was they'd come to be here, and Jamshed, with his customary polite inscrutability, said, 'Yes, sir.'

That night Byrd stood in front of his bedroom mirror looking at his naked body. It was long and thin and the skin in places was droopy where it had lost its youthful elasticity. He found himself thinking of the dry, wrinkled eucalyptus seeds in the saddlebags of the soldiers' horses and in the pockets of their military coats, rattling up into the mountains and taking root here in the damp mountain soil and flourishing. He put his hand on his chest and he could feel his heart beating.

What was it that Mann had written?

A late adventure of the feelings – something like that.

39

She hadn't known he was there, the time he'd come and stood next to her at the market.

She was right in the middle of stealing *The Best of Bonnie Raitt*, and suddenly there he was, so close his shoulder was almost touching hers. She'd held her breath and didn't move. She had the plastic case half in and half out of her sleeve because this was what she did now: stole a new CD every week, took it home, slit the clear wrapper open with Aunty's sharpest knife, listened to the songs over and over in secret while Aunty was out, then taped the wrapper up as invisibly as possible over the plastic case and brought it back to the stall, like a library book. With the boy at her shoulder she didn't know what the best thing would be to do – to push the CD further into her kurti, or let it slide back onto the higgledy-piggledy pile with all the others. Her scalp fizzed and shrank. Her blood turned cold. As the boy moved even closer she waited to hear herself declared a thief. Instead, he tapped the edge of the CD case through her sleeve and said in a fierce whisper, 'This one is *so* good!'

The next time she was there he pushed Garth Brooks' *Ultimate Hits* towards her across the top of the pile then struck up a loud diversionary conversation with the stall owner while she slipped it into her sleeve and left. The third time he asked her, over the top of the undulating heaps of CDs, who was her

Number One between Johnny Cash and Lyle Lovett? When she said Lyle Lovett he threw his arms up in the air and shouted, in English, 'No way!' Then he started singing. He was over on her side of the stall by now and it was a Johnny Cash song she'd heard before. She couldn't remember the title but it was something to do with a murder and a train, and like almost all the Country music she knew, the melody was beautiful and sad. The boy's voice was a little reedy, but warmer and lower than she'd have expected it to be, coming out of so thin a body. For the first time she looked at him properly.

His moustache really was very big – much too big for his sharp and narrow face, and the white cowboy hat was a ridiculous thing which made him look as if he thought he was an *actual* Country and Western singer.

These were the two things she hung onto in the weeks that followed – when she returned to the stall where, sooner or later, the boy always turned up.

She clung to the fact of his moustache being too big and his hat being ridiculous, because she knew from her time at Aunty's, after the boys came, how miserable you could be if you allowed yourself to have feelings which weren't returned. She knew that you had to shut yourself off and smother your emotions – that you had to protect yourself because no one else would. But as the weeks passed and she kept going back to the stall and the boy kept on being there, it became impossible for Priscilla to persuade herself that either the moustache or the hat was in any way unappealing.

Under the awning at the far end of the stall they swapped snatches of their favourite songs. Early on, they agreed they didn't much care for the ones which went on too much about

God or Jesus, however lovely the melodies were – the ones with what Ravi called 'too much Hallelujah'. As for the rest, if they knew the words, or at least a rough approximation of them, they sang them, the beautiful phrases about night winds whispering and burning rings of fire and weeping willows and eyes wide open and this heart of mine. And if they didn't know the words, they hummed, sometimes together and sometimes alone while the other listened, leaning in a little to catch the tune over the din of the market, nodding and saying, 'Who's this one by?' or 'Yes, yes, I love this one.'

In between the singing and the humming Ravi told Priscilla about the car crash he'd been too young to remember which had killed his parents; about his life with his mother's sister who'd fed him and clothed him and sent him to school and given him a home since he was three years old in one of the apartments over by the old racecourse; about his uncle who was his father's older brother and was completely against him becoming a Country and Western singer. Priscilla in turn told Ravi how her mother had hidden her in the bushes beside the lake until one day she was found by Aunty, and that she'd lived at Aunty's ever since. Ravi asked her if she remembered her mother and she said no, not at all. She wished she did but she didn't. And when he asked her how she'd lost her thumbs, she told him she didn't lose them, she'd never had them – to which Ravi *didn't* say (as one of the foreign volunteers at Aunty's had once observed) that he supposed you couldn't miss what you'd never had.

Priscilla thought that might have been the precise moment when she started to really love Ravi – to really, *really* love him.

◆

And what of Ravi?

Ravi, it has to be said, was a little slower on the uptake.

It was fun when the girl with no thumbs started turning up at the market stall, stealing all the CDs which, if he'd been making a list of CDs to steal, would have been pretty much the exact same ones he'd have chosen. But what did it mean, exactly, to Ravi? That it was 'fun'? Was it because he'd found something he'd never had before – an audience? Was it the thrill he experienced when he sang *Folsom Prison Blues* to Priscilla and she seemed so moved he thought she was going to cry? Was it because he'd discovered an audience that he found himself looking out of the window of the CTR salon every five minutes during the weeks which followed, to see if she was there again? Was it because, until now, the only audience he'd ever had was the wall of mirrors in the salon late at night when he'd been left to lock up?

Or was it, rather, that in Priscilla he had found a person who took him seriously? A person who told him he had a good voice, and that she liked his hat, but who also said he had a long way to go if he was ever going to be an actual Country and Western singer. A person who, when he told her he was learning to play the guitar without yet owning a guitar by watching someone on YouTube, said she thought that was a very good idea, he just needed to keep on with it.

Was it perhaps that for Ravi, being taken seriously was a necessary condition for the beginning of love?

◆

It was a shock, and he hardly knew what had hit him, when suddenly the girl with no thumbs vanished.

Every time he looked up and out through the window of the CTR salon, hoping to see her at the stall, picking her way through the CDs, she wasn't there.

He wandered around the town hoping to bump into her but he never did.

Already thin, he grew thinner.

He didn't know that, out of the blue, Aunty had told Priscilla she was going to be living with the Padre from now on, and that Priscilla, though she often came into town with the Padre, had so far found it impossible to slip away even for five minutes by herself.

By the time he was sweeping the leaves from Miss Moreland's lawn one Tuesday evening and saw Priscilla walking up the drive with a fat old man in a scarf and a too-large fleece hat, Ravi was miserable and ill. He stood with his broom and willed her to look over at him but she didn't, she carried on walking in her brisk, distinctive way all the way up to the house with the fat old man he now recognised was the Padre who occasionally came to visit Miss Moreland.

The rest was very quick.

In the kitchen he helped himself to a glass of water from the tap. Through the open door he heard the chink of tea cups from the interior of the house. He heard Miss Moreland and the Padre having one of their slightly bad-tempered conversations; he heard the Padre saying it would be helpful if she could play a little faster during the Sunday morning service; he heard Miss Moreland say, 'Priscilla, would you take the tray out to the kitchen, I think we're finished here'; he heard Priscilla's quick, light-then-heavy step on the wooden floor in the hallway and by the time she reached him he was already singing softly to her from just behind the door.

40

'Mr Byrd, come quickly! I have good news!'

The Padre was standing at the front door of the presbytery. His eyes twinkled and he was smiling. He spoke in an excited whisper.

'Quickly, Mr Byrd, in here.'

Inside the drawing room the Padre closed the door. He glanced at the paper parcel of cloth under Hilary Byrd's arm.

'Mr Byrd, tonight I think we will postpone our sewing lesson because I do not think it will be possible for us to concentrate.'

Byrd inclined his head. The Padre was beaming and a sick presentiment prevented Byrd from speaking. He could think of only one thing, one single piece of good news, which could have produced such excitement in the old clergyman.

He shifted the parcel of cloth from under his right arm to his left and waited. The Padre leaned in closer. Byrd swallowed. 'Mr Byrd,' said the Padre. 'I believe God has sent us a husband for Priscilla.' His eyes were moist with emotion, and Byrd waited for him to describe the boy he had at last found for Priscilla. 'He is' – the old clergyman began, smiling broadly – 'a little old for her perhaps, but I do not think this is a problem.'

Byrd blinked. His heart bounced. He swallowed again and stood without speaking. It seemed almost possible – he could almost believe the Padre was right, that he *had* been brought here by some sort of weird destiny. By the appalling heat of the plains, by the overheard conversation of the German tourists, by his accidental meeting with the Padre on the train – that all of it had been somehow ordained, meant. He could hardly breathe. 'Yes,' continued the Padre. 'We will have a meeting, and if it all goes well, he will speak to her afterwards on the telephone.'

The strangeness of this last sentence wrapped itself around Byrd's heart like a cold cloth.

By telephone?

He clutched for a straw of logic. Perhaps this was how it was done here? A period of time where he and Priscilla would be expected to remain apart and only communicate by phone?

'Yes, Mr Byrd,' said the Padre. 'He will be here tomorrow. A good boy from Mettupalayam. A little old for her, as I said, but he has been waiting a long time for his elder brother to marry first. He is coming with his mother on the 12 o'clock train.'

Byrd opened his mouth and closed it again. 'Have you told Priscilla?' It was all he could think of to say.

'Of course!'

The Padre patted Byrd lightly on the arm. He was beaming still. 'Tell me this, Mr Byrd, tomorrow when the boy comes with his mother, will you make scones for us?'

41

Something has happened again to Mr Byrd, wrote Jamshed.

It was like before, a few weeks ago, when Mr Byrd's bright cheerfulness had vanished overnight. His long face in the rear-view mirror suddenly anxious and unhappy.

All day today, Mr Byrd had sat without speaking in the back of the auto while they drove about. He'd gone to the Nazri Hotel for his lunch. Then he asked to go to the lake, and it was nothing like the last time, when he'd been so cheerful and full of smiles and had asked Jamshed to come with him. This time he climbed wordlessly out of the cab. This time at the kiosk he paid for a boat and rowed it out, and when he reached the middle of the lake he stopped and opened his black umbrella and sat beneath it without moving, crouching in the cold and drifting on the dark surface of the water. His was the only boat, and from the cab the only sound Jamshed could hear was the faraway plopping of raindrops falling. Mr Byrd held the curved handle of the umbrella with both his hands. The oars drooped in the rowlocks, the paddles disappeared under the water. Once in a while, a light, damp wind filled the boat's black umbrella sail and pushed it along. From the shore, Jamshed watched it float further and further out across the miserable lake. How sad and solitary Mr Byrd looked! A tiny, humped figure in the distance.

✦

Jamshed described the scene as best he could in his soft-covered exercise book.

For a long time, in his hut, he replayed it all in his memory. Then he walked down to the river and sat by himself on a stone and had a smoke. It was as if, since yesterday, a kind of veil had come down between them. Mr Byrd's invitation to come out with him onto the lake seemed like something from another world. Was he just having one of his bad days, or was there something on his mind?

Some story in his head perhaps (wrote Jamshed) *he is not telling.*

42

When the scones were ready, Priscilla arranged them, as she had the first time they'd made them, on a white plate, and spooned raspberry jam into the small yellow bowl.

The Padre paced up and down. Byrd had never seen him so agitated.

He was bustling nervously about, smoothing his bald head with his palm; walking out of the room and back into it again; telling Priscilla to fetch another jug of water because this one wasn't cold enough; changing his trousers; rushing off to make some slight alteration to Priscilla's résumé; saying quietly to Hilary Byrd that he was worried about her having neither a birth certificate nor a school certificate, that he didn't know if, after all, the task ahead was a small one or a large one but they would soon find out. He was a little anxious still, about the mother – the boy himself by all accounts was in no way opposed to marrying an orphan, but the mother … His voice trailed off as his gaze moved over the plate of scones and the small ceramic pots of jam and butter, and Byrd, as he stood watching, clutched at this sudden straw: that the mother might prevent it all. But then the Padre gave himself a little shake, as if the inviting tea-time spread had calmed his fears and given him a reviving boost. He winked at Hilary Byrd, and when he spoke again his voice was jocular and light. Weren't all mothers the same when it came down to it? Was there a mother anywhere in the world who thought a girl could ever be good enough for her son?

As for Priscilla, she wore the trousers and tunic they had made out of a length of mustard-coloured cloth with a pattern of sparkling flowers he had bought in the market. Her hair gleamed with oil and there was a new cream leather shoe on her good foot. Byrd watched her stumping about, sweeping the wide wooden floorboards with a short-handled brush, bent over with one hand behind her back. There was a fresh cloth on the heavy mahogany table in the middle of the room, pink asters and orange gladioli in a tall white vase; four chairs. Ah, well that was one good thing at least: he was not expected to stay. It would be the Padre and the boy and the boy's mother and Priscilla, and he would hear all about it, he supposed, later.

Priscilla was giving the ancient upright piano a vigorous polish now and he couldn't see her face.

'Priscilla?' he said softly, stepping towards her across the thread-bare carpet.

But Priscilla had begun the noisy work of wiping the piano keys and an ugly plinking filled the room, and she didn't answer him or look up. Her thumbless hand gripped the cleaning rag, her front teeth pressed down firmly into her bottom lip. When she moved he heard the squeak of her new shoe.

'You look lovely, Priscilla,' he said but she still didn't look up.

'Well,' he said, not knowing what else to say, 'I'll leave you to it.'

43

Jamshed shook his head but he was smiling, proud.

'Look at you, boy! Like proper cowboy. Like Lee Van Cleef or Charlton Heston. All you need now is a gun.'

The two men – the old one and the young one, the uncle and the nephew – stood in the evening twilight outside the back of the CTR salon, looking at the horse beneath the tin awning. This was where the scrawny animal stayed while Ravi was working; Ravi paid the salon owner half his wages and though the owner had complained at first about the horsey smell, there was something amusing about the sight of the horse's head looking into the salon through the back window. The customers seemed to enjoy it and the owner, in the end, seemed happy with the arrangement.

'Maybe Stephen,' said the old driver.

Ravi pulled a face. He had wondered at first about an American name for the horse, the name of one the great men themselves, Johnny or Lyle or Garth or Randy, but he'd tried these out on the horse and the horse had looked back at him sadly.

After that he'd tried out his father's name, Bipin, because even though Ravi had no memory of his father, his name brought with it feelings of warmth and safety. But the horse hadn't recognised itself in the two short syllables of Bipin, any more than it had in Johnny or Lyle or Randy or Garth.

What sort of name would Ravi prefer? asked Jamshed. An American one or an Indian one? Ravi said he didn't care what kind of name it was or where it came from, so long as the horse liked it. It could be Spanish for all he cared, or Chinese. What was the name of the Englishman he drove around all day, the one who'd come in the other day to the salon?

Jamshed said this man's name was Mr Byrd.

'Yes, Uncle, but what's his other name?'

By now Jamshed knew Hilary Byrd's full name because it had tumbled out in several of the stories Byrd had told about himself as they rattled around the town together, but Jamshed didn't like the idea of Mr Byrd's name being given to a horse, so he lied and said he didn't know and repeated his earlier suggestion – 'Maybe Stephen.'

Stephen was the name of the headmaster at the expensive boarding school in town who attended the Tuesday evening Bible class at the house of Miss Moreland, the Australian organist from St Peter's church, whose garden Ravi swept on Tuesdays and Thursdays when he was finished cutting hair and trimming beards and shaving. Jamshed, because he had sometimes driven the headmaster to Miss Moreland's house, had heard the Australian spinster call him *Stephen*.

His uncle's suggestion made Ravi think about the names of the two other foreigners who attended Miss Moreland's class on a Tuesday. One was Gerald and the other was Rob.

Ravi walked around the thin, newly purchased animal which stood now beneath the tin porch at the back of the CTR salon. 'No way Gerald,' he said aloud to his uncle in English. Gerald came sometimes to sit in the garden and drink gin with Miss Moreland. Gerald was the old fart who waved his walking stick in the air and pointed out wattle and eucalyptus leaves and pine needles Ravi had missed with his broom and called him 'young chota wallah'.

Jamshed produced a banana from his pocket and began to peel it for the horse.

Had Ravi been aware of the trouble today in town? he asked his nephew. No, said Ravi. What trouble?

He was still walking around the horse, thoughtful and preoccupied. 'Hello, Rob,' he whispered experimentally, but the thin horse only stared at the ground.

Jamshed broke off a piece of banana so the horse could take it from his hand. He said that while he was waiting for Mr Byrd to come out of the Botanical Gardens, a taxi driver had been pulled out from his cab and beaten. The driver's vehicle was decorated inside like a church – on the dashboard a big picture of Jesus Christ, garlanded like a Formula One star with blossoms and lit from beneath with a red electric candle. He was beaten pretty badly.

Ravi clucked his tongue. 'Idiots,' he said, switching to his own language. 'All of them.' What difference did they think it made if you crouched in front of a little arrangement of empty coconut shells in a roadside shrine opposite the Bharat Petroleum Station, or if you knelt beneath the coloured glass windows of St Peter's church? None! None at all!

Jamshed nodded. He couldn't help smiling. He liked it when his nephew echoed his own opinions so exactly. It made him feel close to him. It made him feel he had at least had some influence on the person Ravi was growing up to be.

The boy was stroking the animal's nose and folding its ears inside his palms then letting them go so they sprang up, tall and alert and pointed, like two finely shaped leaves, soft and pink on one side, furry and grey on the other. He ruffled the animal's straggly fringe and smoothed its long neck with the palm of his hand but didn't speak, and for a while it seemed that the horse would remain nameless.

Then Ravi, a little tentatively, a little – it has to be said – doubtfully, whispered, 'Hello there, Stephen,' and this time the horse's tall leaf-like ears moved forward in unison and its lips made a long flubbering sound of pleasure and satisfaction.

The old man nodded. 'There, boy,' he said. 'Maybe Stephen.'

44

Byrd was in bed when the Padre knocked at his bungalow door to tell him the scones had been a great success. The boy had eaten two, the mother five.

He'd been very hopeful this time, he said.

However, the boy had not called this evening, and he had not heard from the mother. That had been the arrangement – that the boy would call on the phone and speak again to Priscilla. But he hadn't, and the Padre did not think now that he would phone. It was a pity. He'd seemed like a good boy. Perhaps, he said, Priscilla had not been what he and his mother were expecting.

Byrd stood in his pyjamas. His heart was beating very fast. He said he was sorry to hear that. The Padre shrugged. He looked sad and very tired. 'I only wanted you to know in case Priscilla seemed a little down in the dumps, and to thank you for the scones.'

Byrd didn't know what to say. The whole thing felt like a reprieve. He wondered if he should tell the Padre everything, get him on his side.

'You'll find someone I'm sure,' he said.

The Padre nodded.

He heard Vallie's voice in his head.

You have to be patient, Pa.

It was what she'd said with Ada – that the right husband

for their daughter would come along when the moment was right, and wasn't that exactly what had happened? Ada had found Jerome by herself, in America: the finest, most educated, most loveable Christian boy.

'Yes, Mr Byrd. I'm sure you are right.' His gloomy expression cleared a little. 'Thank you, yes, I hope so. Seek and we shall find, yes indeed. A good Christian boy.'

The edge of the old rug under Byrd's feet felt precipitous suddenly, as if he might be about to fall again, as he had all those weeks ago from the top of the greasy steps in the market. He could not have been more taken aback if the Padre had punched him in the face.

'Christian?'

The Padre tilted his head to one side as if puzzled; as if his English visitor had asked the strangest and most unexpected of questions – a question to which the answer was so obvious and self-evident and transparently clear, it hardly needed an answer.

'Of course, Mr Byrd. Only a good Christian husband for my darling, darling girl.'

45

On the front cover of his graph-paper exercise book, Jamshed, in due course, will write:

Story of Mr Byrd

Because it will seem to him that this is what they are amounting to, his daily handwritten entries on the graph-paper pages. His record of the time he's been spending with Mr Hilary Byrd from Petts Wood UK. His account of the beginning and the middle, but not yet the end.

His account of how the Englishman let him boil water for a hot water bottle and tuck him up in bed.

His account of how he let him build a sweet-smelling fire and offer him a cold bag of milk to press against his injured face; how, after his fall, he insisted on using no other driver; how almost every morning at 9.15 for weeks he insisted Jamshed wait for him at the bottom of the steps in his auto and drive him, day after day, all over town, everywhere he wanted to go.

His account of how he listened to Hilary Byrd talk about various incidents in his life, his feelings of lowness and depression.

His account of how he, Jamshed, became aware of something changing; that there were certain important things Mr Byrd was not talking about.

His account of how Hilary Byrd went from telling him everything to telling him nothing.

46

Byrd climbed into the back of the auto and the old man, hunched over the wheel, manoeuvred them into the traffic.

The weather had become warmer, these past few days, and drier, but today a cold wind blew in through the open side of the cab, making the old driver's WORLD CLASS shirt billow like a faded spinnaker. From time to time he squeezed the green rubber horn, making the small, sad sound which reminded Byrd of his old toy mouse.

He told Jamshed to drive and not stop anywhere. They passed all Byrd's usual haunts and at each one Jamshed slowed in case Mr Byrd decided he did, after all, want to stop. But in the back of the auto Byrd sat without moving.

He had not slept after the Padre's visit.

After a long time he asked suddenly, 'Are you religious at all, Jamshed?'

The old driver looked up into the rear-view mirror. 'Sir?'

'Are you religious? Are you Christian, Hindu, Muslim? Zoroastrian? Buddhist?'

The old man shook his head. 'No, sir. Own head, own heart, own feet, own stomach. Ourselves only. Nothing else, sir. One life, this life.'

Byrd nodded, and for a while they drove in silence.

'*Christian?*' he heard himself say again.

It had come out of him like a squeak.

Of course, Mr Byrd. Only a good Christian husband for my darling, darling girl.

He thought of his very first dinner with the Padre in the presbytery, not long after his arrival, when Priscilla had appeared for the first time. He thought of the fish and the salted limes.

He thought of the Padre asking him, when they had almost finished eating, 'You are a Christian, Mr Byrd?'

His emphatic, 'Lord, no!'

Through the open side of the clattering auto he watched the world go bouncing past. They sped past the tall iron railings of the Botanical Gardens. Past the internet cafe and the Savoy and the eastern entrance to the market. Every once in a while he glimpsed Jamshed's dark eyes looking at him in the rear-view mirror, as if the old man expected him at any moment to tell him to pull over and announce that he was getting out. But Byrd didn't tell Jamshed to pull over. He didn't say anything. He sat folded up on the back seat. He shifted his long legs and pushed aside a thin strand of hair which drooped down onto his nose. What a mess he had made of everything. What a fool he was to have thought the Padre had ever considered him as a possible suitor. What an idiot he was for excluding himself so irrevocably from the running, right at the start, with his 'Lord, no!' He closed his eyes and allowed himself to be jostled from side to side by the racing auto.

Well, he would not give up.

He would pretend.

Yes. He would do everything necessary to make himself suitable in the Padre's eyes, and while all that was happening he would hope – pray! – that Priscilla liked him at least a little, and that bit by bit she'd come to like him more and more. If the Padre questioned him about his beliefs, he'd say it was his fall – his terrible plunge down the greasy rain-slick steps outside the market which had hurled him into the road and nearly killed him. He'd say it had changed him.

The grace from his primary school came back to him. He could hear the hurried rote chant which preceded the screech of benches being pushed back in the cavernous dining hall which echoed like a swimming pool, a hundred children sitting thunderously down to eat. *For what we are about to receive may the Lord make us truly thankful. Amen.*

None of it was unfamiliar. He knew the Bible, the Book of Common Prayer. All the Moveable Feasts.

He knew how to kneel. He would do pretty well in any sort of test, if the Padre chose to put him through anything like that. Like everyone his age, he'd been brought up in school on a diet of hymns and prayers. Every year the calendar had been punctuated with Lent and Easter and Christmas, with carol services and nativities. He knew the names of all the disciples, the stories of Cain and Abel and Noah, he knew the names of Noah's sons, the stories of Job, and Lazarus, and Lot's wife, the flight to Egypt and the man born blind, the parables of the mustard seed and the talents. He knew about the Sea of Glass in the Book of Revelation, he could recite part of the Song of Solomon and the twenty-third Psalm. He would not fail, he was sure. He would make a convincing-enough Christian.

He leaned forward and told Jamshed, over the rumble and clatter of the traffic, that he was ready to go home, there was nowhere he wanted to stop today.

Later, through the window of his bungalow, on the far side

of the lawn, he saw Priscilla emerge from the trees beyond the perimeter of the garden and make her brisk, lopsided way past the roses and the hydrangea and the banana tree. In the sunshine the spangled yoke of her new tunic sparkled. He watched her all the way into the house until she closed the door and disappeared.

47

More and more often these days, in the evenings when Priscilla had gone to bed and Ooly was quiet in her sink next to the boiler house and Mr Byrd had turned out the lights in the mission house, the Padre drifted into dreams about his dead wife. He felt lost and melancholy, sitting alone at his desk munching on a bowl of fryums and looking out through the old French windows into the darkness of the presbytery garden, wishing they had not had the stupid argument, that final morning, about the leopard.

'No,' he'd said, chuckling and shaking his head when Vallie claimed she'd just seen one in the garden. No sensible leopard, he'd insisted, would come stepping out of the forest of its own accord in the middle of the morning. The only leopard either of them was likely to see in town was the one whose dusty head was mounted on the wall in the library with all the other creatures the British had found to hunt when they came and made the place their own.

He had continued to laugh and shake his head in what he could see now had been an irritating way. 'No, no, no, Vallie. A leopard. Oh no. I don't think so.'

And Vallie *had* been irritated. Irritated and cross.

'I saw it, Pa. Right there.' She'd pointed, out into the garden towards the far border where the lawn met the tree line. 'I saw it. It was sitting there. It was a leopard. I saw it.'

The Padre, still chuckling, had said it would have been one of the wild dogs from the railway tracks, or some other wild dog from some other place.

'Well,' said Vallie. 'I know what I saw,' and in the middle of that night she'd had her stroke and the following afternoon he'd made the terrible phone call to Ada in California. All morning he'd sat by the phone unable to pick it up, rehearsing what he would say, calling her, in the end, in the middle of the Californian night. 'I am sorry, little one, to wake you. Your mummy died. Yes. My Vallie. I know.' He would give anything now not to have been so annoying about the leopard. He would give anything not to have scoffed like that, for it not to have been their last ever conversation.

Looking out now into the darkness of the garden, he told Vallie about the set-back they'd had the other week with the boy from Mettupalayam and his mother. It had, he said, been something of a disaster. But they had put it behind them, and they were pressing on with the reading and the writing with Mr Hilary Byrd, the needlework and the baking, and it all seemed to be going very well. He only wished she was here to help him with everything. He was still so unsure about what he was doing and whether it would all turn out all right.

Later, Ada phoned.

She chatted about her students and the new apartment they'd been to see in Petaluma and might be able to buy if she and Jerome both made associate professor. 'There'd be a room for you, Daddy.'

'Ah!' laughed the Padre, and called his daughter incorrigible, and said thank you, but he was very well for the moment where he was.

'But I worry about you, Daddy.'

She was always reading things on the internet, he knew that. He knew almost nothing was ever reported in the American papers, but the internet was full of things and they never seemed to escape his faraway daughter.

It was nothing to worry about, he said. Nothing too bad had happened for a good while now and anyway it was all different up here in the hills, she knew that as well as he did. Here, everything was peaceful.

'Everywhere's peaceful until it isn't, Daddy,' said Ada. 'Just because you don't notice the cracks it doesn't mean they aren't there.'

That night he dreamed he was beaten with sticks by men whose faces he couldn't see, that he was hung from a tree with a bicycle chain and set on fire. He woke in a bath of sweat, and when Mr Byrd came for supper he couldn't help puffing out his cheeks and shaking his head and saying that he was afraid his country was in trouble. Was the UK also in trouble? he asked, munching rapidly on a handful of fryums. People wanting to be surrounded only by people who were the same as they were? Wanting to travel back in time to a golden place? He told Mr Byrd about the beatings and the burnings, the lynchings and the riots, and Hilary Byrd looked up from his plate. There was an absent look on his face, as if he was not quite present and had more important matters on his mind. Was the UK in trouble? Byrd said he didn't know, he wasn't sure. Everyone seemed excited about the Olympics – very happy and proud and patriotic – but beyond that, he couldn't say. It was a long time since he'd travelled anywhere beyond Petts Wood, and that seemed like a peaceful enough place.

48

It was years, decades, since Hilary Byrd had set foot in a church to attend any kind of service.

Up ahead, near the front, he could see Priscilla. Someone handed him a maroon hymnal and a brown and turquoise Book of Common Worship. He sang and chanted with the rest of them. He watched the Padre turn his eyes to the ceiling when Miss Moreland, the Australian organist, began to play, a steady two beats behind the singing of the congregation.

There was a long, stained-glass window Byrd knew must depict Jacob's Ladder; another which must be Moses, because the figure had horns, and Byrd knew that this often happened to Moses – he remembered it from school, that Moses was often depicted as something he wasn't, because of a mistranslation from the Hebrew, 'blazing with light' having been translated as 'with horns'.

He watched Priscilla bow her head, zip and unzip her Bible. When the time came for a new hymn he closed his eyes, because he could hear her voice, unexpectedly strong and lovely, above all the others. He found himself looking around at all the other men, young and old, afraid now that one of them might come forward, either by themselves or at the Padre's prompting, as a possible suitor. Suddenly it seemed possible that everything would change now, and that Priscilla, instead of being someone no one wanted, would be someone everyone wanted.

The Padre was in the pulpit now, reading the notices for the coming week – the times and places for the choir to practise, for the Bible study group to meet. He instructed anyone planning to marry, and requiring the banns to be read, to apply directly to the presbytery.

Byrd pictured a queue of youngish men lined up along the puddled red driveway.

Priscilla shouting, 'No, no!' at the Padre, and stamping her heavy leather boot on the faded paisley carpet. 'I choose Mr Byrd!'

As she passed him she smiled. 'Hello, Uncle. Coming to church now?'

Was she teasing him?

It was impossible to tell.

In the evenings, when they were together in the presbytery under the Padre's supervision, she was eager and enthusiastic. Baking or cutting out and sewing, transforming the patterned lengths of fabric Byrd bought in the market into the things she wanted. In a few short hours, between the two of them, changing nothing into something.

When she read to him she was earnest and studious, but although she did not seem in any way to shy away from him, she didn't look up, either, at his face. She had passed him no more tiny mysterious notes when the Padre was out of the room. All her effort and concentration were focussed on the shapes of the words on the illustrated pages. Going to sleep for a hundred years, turning pumpkins into glass coaches, spinning straw into gold.

It was impossible to tell if she had feelings but was hiding them.

Every time she called him *Uncle* now, it hurt his heart.

The church *was* beautiful – a long, narrow-shouldered structure with a delicate white spire that seemed to disappear when you looked up into the misty clouds; its jewelled windows shone and the whole thing was set like a precious stone in the centre of the grassy churchyard which was dotted all over with the tranquil grey of speckled graves.

It made him uncomfortable, all the pretending. How nice it would be to sit inside the church in one of the pews or on one of the rush-seated chairs, or stand on the steps at the big oak doors and peer into the softly illuminated darkness and feel belief sink into him like rain. It would make everything easier. But belief didn't sink into him like rain, and it all still seemed to him, more or less, like nonsense. In all of it – in the rows and rows of chairs, and the long red carpet and the patterned windows and the pulpit, in the piles of brick-coloured prayer books and maroon hymnals, in the candlesticks, and the chandeliers hanging from the fishbone roof and all the bright and gilded paraphernalia of the Padre's work, and in the arrangement of grey, speckled stones outside in the churchyard – he saw only the longing of the living, and the continual addition to the legions of the dead who were forever dead.

49

Hilary Byrd looked like a nice man.

He'd come twice now to her house on Tuesday evenings, to take part in the Bible study group. The group was never especially well attended, and Frances Moreland suspected the Padre of discouraging people to come because she'd ticked him off two Christmases ago for eating too many fryums and he had taken offence, which was why she, in turn, was punishing him with her slow organ playing.

There were just eight regular attenders: the Canadian missionary, Mr Henry Page, who was in Canada seeing about his visa; Stephen Thackwray, the headmaster of the expensive boarding school and his wife Connie, who were English; Rob Parks, who was the new buildings supervisor at the school and his wife Jan, who were from Perth, Australia; Murali, whose surname she could never remember, who worked at Higginbotham's bookshop; her friend, Sunitha, who ran the small shop where the Women Workers' Co-operative sold their hand-dyed bed linen and natural cosmetics; and Gerald Cameron, who spoke and dressed like someone who had been asleep or frozen for a hundred years, who carried a walking stick he didn't need and wore knee breeches and a belted wool jacket and a green felt hat with a feather in it and used words like 'ague' and 'decko' and referred to people as 'jossers' and 'jugginses' and to Ravi, who came in on Tuesday and Thursday evenings to gather sticks for her boiler and sweep the leaves in the driveway, as her 'young chota wallah'. Awful man, Cameron was, really, though he made her laugh sometimes.

And now here was Hilary Byrd. Tall, polite, quiet, intelligent, and with whom, tonight, she'd shared such an enjoyable moment of private entertainment.

They had decided, as a group, to return to the Book of Genesis and work their way forward. Stephen Thackwray had been reading. The world was created: the earth and the heavens and the Garden of Eden; Adam, and from Adam's rib, Eve. The serpent had been and gone, and now Adam, in the voice of Stephen Thackwray, was explaining to God why he had eaten of the Tree of the Knowledge of Good and Evil; Adam, in the voice of Stephen Thackwray, was telling God that the woman made him do it.

There was a brief pause during which the headmaster glanced at his wife and looked afraid, as if steeling himself for an attack from her corner of the sofa, but Connie Thackwray was quiet, and so was everyone else; no one seemed to mind Adam putting all the blame on Eve, except for Gerald Cameron, who rapped the ferrule of his walking stick on Frances's wooden floor and stabbed the air shouting, 'Shabby dog! Shabby, shabby dog!'

At which Hilary Byrd stifled a laugh, and Frances caught his eye, and the two of them exchanged a quick conspiratorial snort.

Later, at the door, when they'd finished their biscuits and drunk their tea, Hilary Byrd was the last to leave.

Gerald Cameron waved his walking stick in the air and called out, 'Cheery-pip,' and Frances Moreland said to

Hilary Byrd, 'The Bible's full of quite a few strange bits and pieces, isn't it?'

And they laughed again, both doing their own imitation of Gerald's outraged and really quite surprising, 'Shabby dog!'

As their laughter petered out, Frances said, 'I just do it for the company really, the whole church thing – for the companionship. There's a lot to be said about that part of belonging to a church.'

'Yes,' said Hilary Byrd, 'I can see that,' and Frances Moreland told him he was welcome, any time, to come and borrow any of her great-aunt's books, anything he liked, they were at his disposal if he ever ran out of things to read at the library.

'Thank you,' said Byrd, and then he was gone – off down her short, neatly swept drive and out onto the road, where she could just make out the small dark shape and distant thrumming engine of a yellow auto rickshaw.

50

Byrd wondered if four Sundays at church and three visits to Frances Moreland's Bible study group was enough; if it was in any way convincing – if it was enough, at least, for him to be thought of as a candidate.

The Padre hadn't questioned him about any of it. Only Priscilla, that first Sunday, had seemed a little surprised, with her smile, and her 'Coming to church now, Uncle?'

The Padre was always on the steps of St Peter's when he arrived for the 9.30 service, his arms spread wide. 'Here again, Mr Byrd, sir!' he announced every time, and there was nothing in the way he said it that sounded like a question. Nothing reserved about his, 'Praise the Lord, you are welcome, sir!' He seemed only happy. If he was in any way surprised that Byrd had suddenly started coming to church, he didn't show it. If he'd thought of him before as a heathen, or a lost sheep, or a lost cause, he didn't mention it. He took Byrd by the arm and ushered him in across the threshold and gave him a maroon hymnal and a brown Church of Southern India prayer book and directed him to a pew or a rush-seated chair near the front.

In the evenings at the presbytery they'd made butterfly cakes and a batch of chocolate chip cookies and started on *The Magic Porridge Pot*, and on the cutting out of a kind of felt poncho which Priscilla had designed herself and asked if he would show her how to make.

Meanwhile Byrd was anxious about his hair. It was a long time since he'd looked at it properly and it dismayed him.

How had it become so colourless and thin? When, exactly, had that happened? Glimpsing his reflection in the window of Higginbotham's bookshop, he hardly recognised himself. Outside Modern Stores, he lingered, looking at the young autorickshaw drivers with their thick glossy hair and luxuriant moustaches. Priscilla, he was certain, would call none of them *Uncle*.

At the CTR salon he told Jamshed to wait. He wouldn't be long.

From his seat at the kerb in his little cab, the old driver waved to his nephew, and watched Hilary Byrd step in through the long strips of coloured plastic which hung in the doorway.

From the television on its high shelf in the corner, the cricket commentary drifted languidly across the shop. India were doing very badly against England, Dravid out for 18 (caught Prior, bowled Anderson). Leaning back against the worn and grainy leather of the barber's chair, not wanting to comment on the cricket in case he appeared to be crowing, Byrd complimented the young hairdresser, instead, on his hat, which was a large white Stetson.

The boy beamed, showing big white teeth, though in reality, the appearance of Mr Hilary Byrd in the shop unnerved him. For a terrible moment, Ravi wondered if the Padre had sent him. But all the Englishman said was that he'd like a haircut, and in the end it was fun, in a dangerously exciting way, to tell him something, if not everything, about his plans.

The hat, he told Hilary Byrd, was part of his costume: he was a Country and Western singer. He had just bought a horse, which would be part of his act, his whole *look*, and Hilary Byrd saw then, through the open door at the back of the salon in a dark lean-to, that there was indeed, munching on a pile of vegetable peelings, a thin grey horse. As soon as the small wound on the horse's leg was completely better, said the boy, he'd be off, down to the plains, where he'd be seeking his fortune playing at weddings and parties at the big hotels in the cities. When he'd made enough money, he would buy himself an apartment in Chennai. He snipped the air with the points of his scissors and grinned. 'No more cutting hair.'

Byrd looked at the boy in the mirror. He had a narrow face and a carefully oiled moustache and seemed to be about twenty-five years old, though he couldn't be sure. He found it difficult to judge the age of anyone under forty. He contemplated his own reflection. He'd been letting his beard grow a little, but it was disappointingly patchy and even when the young barber finished trimming it, it still looked variegated and strange. Wisps of hair from above his ears drifted like feathers onto his shoulders and floated to the floor, and he waited for the hoped-for improvement in his appearance, but there was none. If anything, it was worse than before, and it felt like an ambush, completely unexpected and absolutely unstoppable, when his tears came. He blinked rapidly, trying to bat away the salty water. He pulled at his nose with his fingers and thumb, and coughed, horrified to be trapped in the grainy leather chair in his nylon gown with the boy's cheerful gaze upon him and no means of escape, though if the boy noticed his distress, he gave no sign.

◆

In the back of Jamshed's auto rickshaw, Byrd sat silently. Once or twice he glimpsed his own image in the rear-view mirror and closed his eyes. Eventually he found himself telling the old man about the young barber who'd cut his hair and trimmed his beard, whose dream it was to be a Country and Western singer in the big hotels in the cities down on the plains; about the boy's white Stetson; his horse.

'Yes, sir,' said the old man. 'This boy is called Ravi.'

'That's right. Ravi. He said his name was Ravi.'

'My nephew, sir.'

'Really?'

'Yes, sir.'

And just for a moment, Hilary Byrd was taken outside himself. Just for a moment, he sat looking at the shiny, spotted skin on the back of Jamshed's head. He had never, in all the weeks he'd been riding around in the old man's auto rickshaw, thought about the old man's life beyond what he'd seen of it.

'Do you have a large family, Jamshed?'

'No, sir. Only nephew.'

51

The horse had put on a considerable amount of weight since Ravi bought it. The hole in its thigh had healed up with a short pink scar.

Early in the mornings the young barber walked it along the main road, out as far as the Bharat Petroleum Station and back again. Now that it was so much stronger and healthier he would have liked to take it for a trot on the old racecourse, but people were planting vegetables there and they would be cross, no doubt, if he got in their way.

He thought about it a lot – arriving on the horse wherever they played. With the horse, they would make a splash.

Even his uncle, who'd been so rude about the horse at the beginning, was nice to Stephen now, and brought him nuts and fruit and various snacks and other tidbits from the market. These days his uncle patted Stephen's neck when he came, and said how much better the horse looked now that he wasn't eating garbage any more. He said he hoped Stephen would like the bright lights of the city and would enjoy all the singing and the dancing.

Ravi would like to tell his uncle about Priscilla. But everything had become so wound up together into such a tight connected ball, it seemed impossible now to say anything. If his uncle said something to the tall Englishman, if the tall Englishman said something to the Padre … best to say nothing. Cutting the Englishman's hair the other day, talking to him about his plans – he'd been so excited and nervous he'd almost dropped his scissors, his hand was so slippery with sweat.

Meanwhile he was worried about his English. Speaking was fine – what he hadn't picked up from the TV, he'd picked up from his uncle. He wished he knew how to read or write some of it though, because he thought they would need that. For posters and fliers and so forth. It would be good, he thought, to have those in English. Also, he wanted to be sure he'd got the words right, when he sang them. He sang what he heard but he was worried he might not have things right. Priscilla was better at that side of things, from living first with Aunty and then with the Padre, who almost always spoke English. Priscilla could read things from the Bible, certain parts, and now she was studying with the Englishman, Mr Byrd, who'd been a librarian in the UK. But even Priscilla still made mistakes. Yesterday in the forest behind the presbytery when they sang *Crazy*, the word *trying* still sounded too much like *drying*, and when they'd checked the lyrics of their best Lyle Lovett number they discovered that what they'd been singing for months as *my Aunt Treega* was actually *me and Trigger*. He worried that there might be much worse mistakes they were making and didn't know about. It made him queasy to think of standing up and singing the wrong words and all the people at one of the big hotel weddings laughing and the hotel manager saying, 'Off with you, boy! Off with you, girl! Go home. Go back to the hills where you came from. Go back to cutting hair and cooking.'

Still, Priscilla's English was improving all the time. Plus, she had almost finished her costume.

Ravi brushed the thin whitish-grey hair of Stephen's mane and whispered into his ear that he was looking very handsome and soon he was going to introduce him to Priscilla, and after that it wouldn't be long. Very soon now, the three of them would be on their way.

52

At two o'clock, the rain came.

First the clouds arrived like vast grey duvets, and although at first there wasn't much more than a mist beneath them – a damp, rolling kind of vapour – soon the proper rain began and did not stop.

'Home, please, Jamshed – quickly!' Byrd called out as he hurried through the library gates, one half of him cross because he'd left his washing on the line, the other half hopeful and excited that Priscilla would be there when he got home and they would laugh about it together – about how completely he'd failed, yet again, to read the weather. The last few weeks had continued sunny and quite warm, but it was cold now, and wet once again.

By the time he arrived at the presbytery, the cratered surface of the driveway was already filled with water and all along it there were blood-red puddles.

He dumped his shopping in the kitchen of his bungalow, dropped the thin parcel of cloth he'd bought in the market for the evening's sewing lesson on the dining table, and went out to inspect his clothes. The washing line dipped like a skipping rope under their weight. His shirts and trousers hung from it like dead bodies. He went back inside and fetched the big pink bucket from his bathroom, pulled all his wet things from the line and piled them into the bucket. When a green plastic peg pinged off the waistband of his trousers and caught him in the eye, he turned towards the presbytery, hoping, in spite of the stinging pain, that Priscilla might be watching and they could share the funny side of it, but she wasn't. Only the dog, Ooly, was there, sitting up in her sink, looking alert and curious to see what would happen next.

Inside the square-roomed mission house Byrd tried to light a fire, thinking he could drape his sodden laundry around the place to dry in the warmth, but the sticks he'd brought in from outside were cold and damp and the flame wouldn't take. Though he pushed scrunched-up balls of newspaper in between the smaller twigs and lit them, after a quick bright burst the fire died every time.

He was shivering now, and very cold. In the pink bucket his clothes sank and settled in a twisted heap, heavy and useless as white elephants. The ones he stood up in were soaked through. 'Oh, good heavens,' said Byrd aloud. He stooped and pulled his suitcase out from under his bed and unzipped it and surveyed the light summer shorts and short-sleeved shirts inside. He had not worn any of them since the day he arrived. He peeled off his wet things and put on a pair of shorts and a thin cotton shirt, but even with the quilt from his bed around his shoulders, he was still covered in goose-flesh.

Not since his very first evening had he examined the clothes of the absent missionary.

Lightly, he placed his fingertips on the edge of his bedroom door and pushed it away from the wall.

He lifted the sleeve of the red lumberjack shirt and opened the flap on one of the pockets of the trousers. He patted the pom-pom on the hat. Everything was wonderfully dry to the touch.

He put them on.

It was a strange feeling.

Strange, but also pleasant. He felt younger. Younger and more attractive; even his hair (what could be seen of it in the mirror beneath the knitted hat) looked better.

He would never have known how to bring about the effect himself – what garments to choose in any shop – but he liked it very much, the transformation Henry Page's outfit had brought about.

In the sitting room a small blaze had taken hold at last in the grate, and Byrd began, after wringing them out in his bathroom, to hang up his own wet things in front of the fire's warmth, draping them over the dining table and the green fridge and the Carter's Nest For Rest and the various doors. Then, clad in Henry Page's sporty outdoor gear and carrying the new parcel of cloth for Priscilla, he stepped out into the evening.

From her sink, the dog looked up at him quizzically.

'Don't worry, Ooly, it's only me,' he said to her in a voice that was more cheerful than any she'd heard him use in a while, and she watched as he continued on, almost jauntily, towards the presbytery, along the path across the garden, where all around and above, the rain had stopped and there were no clouds, only the unfamiliar stars whose patterns Byrd did not recognise and would not have been able to identify or name if he'd been asked.

53

In the jewellery district he told the old driver to wait.

On a felt-covered tray, a selection of rings. Was this what was done? A ring? Byrd, his head bowed over the tray, had no idea. There was one with a dark red stone which the owner of the shop insisted was a ruby, and although it quite obviously wasn't, he liked it anyway: the plain setting, the thin silver band decorated with a design of leaves and flowers like the illustrated margin in one of Priscilla's reading books.

He knew it was premature. He wasn't even sure if this was the right way to proceed here, with the offering of a ring. No doubt the old driver would know, but he still couldn't bring himself to tell him about any of it. He felt that if he told anyone – Wyn, or Jamshed – he would be inviting their opinion; their assessment of his chances, or the wisdom of it all, and he didn't want that. It seemed like ages since he'd written to Wyn or sent her an email. As long as he held it all inside himself, his feelings and everything he was doing, it seemed to him as if anything was possible.

So instead of asking the old man what he thought, he'd chuntered away, this morning, about his past, because talking about his past made him feel better, somehow – more confident and optimistic. It reminded him how distant it was now, and of how far he'd come.

He'd talked, as he had so many times in the beginning,

about the alcove of dictionaries at his old library, and what a blow it had been when they were removed because they took up so much space, and nobody was using them any more as they were available, now, on the computers.

The dictionary alcove had been one of his favourite places, he said. He was interested in words, and at quiet moments during the day, he'd enjoyed sitting at the table in the alcove, pulling different dictionaries from the shelves. His favourite one was the Norn one. Norn being a lost language, he told the old driver, once spoken on certain tiny islands off the coast of Scotland.

This bit about the Norn language was new to Jamshed, and he said, 'In UK, sir?'

'Yes, Jamshed.'

Byrd had talked then about the many words there were in Norn for bogs and wool and weather, and about certain words that were forbidden – taboo – at sea, for which the islands' fishermen had replacements because they feared the usual everyday ones would bring bad luck.

'I used to write them down in a notebook, Jamshed – all the ones I liked best – and memorise them. Not just the taboo ones, but the others as well.' *Afrog*, for example, meant 'the backwash of waves that have broken on the shore'. *Brimstew* described 'a dense spray rising from a heavy surf along the coast'. *Torf* was an adjective which meant 'overcast with small dense clouds', while *sid* meant 'to rain softly in calm weather'. *Snisk*, on the other hand, was 'to rain very lightly'. An *onlup* was a downpour. A *bladd* was a very large raindrop.

'I loved them, Jamshed. These lists of words. Their strange and very specific meanings. I felt – I don't know – a kind of sympathy with them I suppose, a sadness, because they were disused and no longer spoken. Only a few of them have survived into the dialect of the present-day islanders. The rest are extinct and understood by no one.'

Jamshed glanced up into the rear-view mirror. Mr Byrd was looking serious and thoughtful.

One of his favourites was the word *horl*, he said, h-o-r-l, which meant 'the rattling noise made by a person with a bad cold'. Another was *doonset*, d-o-o-n-s-e-t, which meant 'a house with a small plot of ground attached'. Then there was also *eterford*, which was 'a bubble of foam on the grass in the hill pasture containing an insect'. 'Don't you love that, Jamshed? That a single word can contain so much meaning?'

Yes, sir, Jamshed was about to say, but then he realised this was only one of Mr Byrd's questions which he asked without really expecting an answer.

'Others I enjoyed just for the sound of them,' he chuntered on. 'Like *glinket*. What do you think *glinket* means, Jamshed?'

The old man shook his head.

'It means "silly, confused, giddy".'

'Glinket,' said Jamshed quietly.

'That's it,' said Hilary Byrd.

And then he was saying how much he liked the word *skrutl*, which meant 'to write very badly' – hence *skrutlins* i.e. something badly written, and perhaps if Byrd had paused then, Jamshed might have confided a little to him about his own skrutlins, but Byrd was absorbed in his reminiscences. 'If I had to choose my favourite word of all, Jamshed, I think it would be *dagwälj*.'

He pronounced it dag-wall-gee, and said it meant 'to work continuously with poor result'.

Jamshed glanced up into the rear-view mirror. Mr Byrd was looking off to the side now, and it was a little while before he spoke.

'I think it's because I used to feel it was what I'd been doing for a long time. Working continuously with poor result. I loved the idea that there were other people who've been alive who needed to describe *exactly* that state of being. It's the sort of word that always made me feel, I don't know, less alone.'

'Yes, sir,' said the old man.

If Jamshed was thinking about whether or not he, too, was alone – if he was thinking about the years he'd spent as a young man, labouring, shovelling lime and gravel and clambering up rickety wooden scaffolds, or all the years since then that he'd been driving his auto rickshaw around the town, taking people to places they needed to go and ferrying them home again; if he was thinking that he, also, for most of his life, had worked continuously with poor result, and that he and Hilary Byrd were perhaps alike in certain ways – he didn't say so. He was quiet.

That night he opened his journal and smoothed a new page with the palm of his hand, thinking about the palace Mr Byrd talked about sometimes that was near his house in Petts Wood and where he often went for walks with his sister. A palace with black swans and a beautiful garden where a young prince called Henry and a pet monkey had once lived. 'You'd like it, Jamshed,' he'd said, and the old man had not been able to shake it off – the idea of being there in the beautiful garden with Mr Byrd, Mr Byrd saying to people, 'This is my friend, Jamshed, all the way from India.'

Doonset, he wrote, = *one house with one small plot of ground attached.*

He put down his ballpoint pen, a picture in his mind of a house with a small plot of ground attached. No one there but Mr Byrd, and him.

For a long time he sat without stirring, thinking of the fishermen Mr Byrd had told him about, setting out in their boats across a cold wide sea, not allowed to speak certain words.

54

'Thank you, Ravi,' said Hilary Byrd.

Every few days now, still clad in the missionary's sporty lightweight gear, he had the old driver drop him at the CTR salon for a shave. In the two weeks that had passed since he visited the jeweller and bought the red-stoned ring, his beard had filled out and thickened and on the whole, he thought, quite significantly improved his appearance, especially now that he was out and about in the missionary's knitted hat. It gave him, he thought, an almost rugged look – made his face more compact somehow, not quite so long and horsey.

It was pleasant, too, to be ministered to by the young barber. He enjoyed the boiling hot flannel Ravi pressed on top of his face, over his mouth and nose and eyes; the drops of eucalyptus oil the boy rubbed into his neck and cheeks. He always left feeling rejuvenated.

He did not feel like an impostor. He didn't feel as if he was pretending to be someone he wasn't. He felt like himself, which is to say, he felt nervous and anxious and sometimes afraid, but also excited and elated and intermittently hopeful and optimistic.

If Priscilla had noticed he was wearing the other man's clothes these days, she didn't say so. Only the Padre, when Byrd stepped in through the presbytery's front door that first time, after the rain, had exclaimed, 'My, what a shock you gave us there, Mr Byrd! For a minute I thought, *What is Mr Page doing back from Canada already? And what has he done with our Mr Byrd?*' But he seemed accustomed now to the change, and to accept Byrd's explanation that none of his own clothes, in spite of all his efforts, were properly dry.

Last night during their reading lesson, Priscilla's eyes had filled suddenly with tears.

She'd been reading *Rumpelstiltskin* to him, quite fluently, and then, abruptly, stopped, glanced quickly at the Padre in the corner, and looked up into Byrd's face.

'Oh, Priscilla,' he'd said, amazed. 'What on earth's the matter?'

She'd shaken her head quickly and rubbed her eyes with her fingers. The words had come out in a rush. 'Wicked lying miller. Cruel ugly gnome. Sad story,' and Byrd couldn't help noticing that, for once, she hadn't called him *Uncle*.

'Don't worry, Priscilla,' he said, his heart galloping. 'Everything turns out all right in the end. Well, not for everyone, not for the gnome, but –' and she'd nodded, and seemed to recover a little, and begun to read again from where she'd left off.

55

It was the only thing about him she didn't love.

She loved his kindness and his patience and the softness of his voice, the way he sometimes lost his train of thought and stood with his arms flung up like a clock, trying to get it back again. She loved the effortful smile that came on his face when he spoke about his wife, and the way his eyes blinked rapidly behind his glasses. She loved the way he let her be part of his irritation with his bossy daughter when she rang from California; the way he asked her every morning if she had slept well; the way he made her feel, always, that she was beloved. The only thing she did not love about him was his obsession with finding her a husband, and his insistence that this husband should be 'a good Christian man'.

Part of her wanted to tell him that she didn't believe in his God, or any other god. Part of her wanted to scream, or laugh, she was never quite sure which, every time she walked home from the wholesaler with him, the two of them carrying their bags of household products and packet stuffs, and they passed the mosques and the Zoroastrians' place and the numerous churches and Hindu temples, and sometimes the Mormon missionaries who came in pairs at different times of the year, always tall and invariably handsome in their dark suits and neatly combed hair, and finally past St Peter's itself on the hill before the presbytery. They were all of them, it seemed to her

– the Mormon boys and the Hindu temples and St Peter's and all the rest of them – the same, like so many shops or market stalls or street traders, all of them hustling for business, all trying to make themselves more appealing than the last one or the next one.

The Padre had explained to her that the British had built St Peter's, just as they had dug the lake and built the railway and the racecourse and the Assembly Rooms and the library and the Botanical Gardens and the Savoy Hotel and Higginbotham's bookshop. But he was also careful to impress upon her that the Christians had been here long before the British came. Jesus's own apostle, Thomas, he told her solemnly, came to the Malabar coast and the Periyar River, where he built churches and converted people. Around the same time, another apostle, called Bartholomew, came too. Some fragments of Bartholomew's head lay now, said the Padre, in Frankfurt cathedral in Germany, and an arm in Canterbury, in the UK.

Part of her wanted to ask if he was sure about that – if there wasn't some other precious piece of his body in a box or a jar anywhere else – a toe in Delhi perhaps, or an eyebrow in London, but she didn't, because she loved him.

Instead she asked about the trouble in Karnataka and Orissa and Gujarat and Uttar Pradesh.

That made the Padre sigh, and look suddenly very tired. Well, he said, that was because after the apostles Thomas and Bartholomew came, so did a lot of foreign missionaries from faraway Christian places like Portugal and Italy, and later from Scotland and England and America and Australia and Canada. 'They came and they built churches, Catholic ones and Protestant ones, and there are those who think we're still too busy converting people. They say we buy their souls with rice and dal.'

'Like the beggars who come to the presbytery gate? The ones we give things to? Like their souls?'

'Like theirs. Yes.'

She almost said, 'Like mine?' just to challenge him, but she didn't, she said, 'Which is why there's trouble?'

The Padre nodded. 'Partly, yes.' He said there was politics mixed up in it too.

She often thought about the two little boys in Orissa, burning inside their father's car. Of all the stories she'd heard or read about or seen on TV it was the one which stuck in her head more than any other. Was it true the boys had been pupils at the expensive boarding school here in town? she'd asked the Padre, and she could see that if he was ever going to lie to her he would have then because he knew it made the whole thing seem very close. He'd been quiet for a while, as if the picture of the burning boys was stuck in his head as firmly as it was in hers. 'They could have been at school anywhere,' he'd said gently. It was just unlucky they were at their father's mission when it happened, and anyway it was a good while ago now.

Well, she had no time for any of it. Any arguing about who had a better claim to be in a place than someone else. Any wrangling over who came first and who came second, any counting of which ones were supposed to be here and which ones weren't. Christian, Buddhist, Muslim, Hindu, Mormon, Zoroastrian, they were all the same as far as she could see. They all thought they were the best, and that God loved their lot more than any other lot. When she was making her slow, laborious way through Mr Byrd's stories in their lessons, it often struck her how much the tales of frogs and princesses, of dark woods and talking mirrors, of spells and wishes and considerable suffering and occasional joy and people doing all kinds of ugly things to each other, resembled the ones in the Bible.

Still, she felt bad about the Padre, guilty.

Yesterday, ploughing through the story about the small gnome and the miller's daughter who was supposed to be able to spin straw into gold, her throat had been so tight, thinking about how she wished she could tell him everything but knowing that she couldn't, she'd had to stop reading. Her eyes had filled up with tears in front of Mr Byrd and she couldn't push the words out. She'd glanced over at the Padre in the corner, his head bent, writing on the big yellow notepad across his lap, and then she'd looked up at Mr Byrd and he'd said, 'Oh, Priscilla, what's the matter?' and she hadn't known what to say. She'd shaken her head quickly and rubbed her eyes with her fingers and snatched at the first lie she could think of. 'Wicked lying miller. Horrible cruel gnome. Sad story.'

Mr Byrd had seemed concerned. He'd told her not to worry. He'd told her everything turned out all right in the end, and that had calmed her somehow. He had a nice voice and she could hear it, still, in her head. If she could find the words, she would like to tell him, this new uncle, about Ravi. This new uncle from Petts Wood UK, who was so helpful and kind and was teaching her so many useful and important new things. How to read and how to write, how to bake and how to sew; how to pronounce the word *Arkansas*.

'You look lovely, Priscilla,' he'd said to her when she was

cleaning the piano before the woman and her son came. She hadn't looked at him. She thought if she looked up at him instead of at the chipped and yellowed keys of the old piano she would burst into tears.

He seemed like someone she could perhaps confide in. This new uncle who'd fallen flat on his face as soon as he'd arrived; this new uncle who always let her beat him at Scrabble.

But then, last week, she'd seen him in church. She hadn't known he was a Christian. He hadn't gone to church in the beginning. She'd thought he was someone who didn't believe in any of that, but now it turned out he did. He would want what the Padre wanted for her, surely.

So she didn't say anything. She'd only looked at him, passing him in his pew, and done her best to smile, and said, 'Coming to church now, Uncle?'

He reminded her of the creatures in the only books she'd liked that Aunty used to have. Written by a doctor from America, they were full of tall, squiggly creatures who were skinny and fat at the same time, mostly with one strand of hair sticking up from the tops of their heads.

Almost every day since he'd arrived, she'd watched him through the window of the presbytery kitchen, walking in the mornings down the steps from the missionary's bungalow past the boiler house and Ooly in her sink on his way into town. Once, looking down into the bungalow from her bedroom, she'd seen him snip open the corner of a bag of milk and try, in one bold movement, to upend it into a metal jug, only to empty the contents all over his lap in a tremendous gush. In the evenings she watched him draw his curtains against the dark, and later saw the slow coil of smoke rising from his chimney.

A few days ago she asked him if he could show her how to make a poncho and he said of course, a poncho would be easy. Just a single piece of felt, and because it was the sort of material that wouldn't fray, they could just cut into it to make the fringes she wanted.

Her costume was almost finished.

Like Ravi's but smaller.

In the evenings, late at night when she wasn't meeting him in the forest and while the Padre was out on his Bun Run, driving around the dark streets near the market on his two-wheeler, distributing bread to people who were hungry, she worked on it – spreading out the piebald cloth Ravi had brought from the market on the big drawing room table, and marking the pattern with the chalk the way Mr Hilary Byrd had taught her in their lessons. Tailor's tacks and seams and darts and hemming; she'd done it all as he'd shown her. Trousers, and a waistcoat to go over her kurti, and the big felt poncho to go over it all.

She won't take anything from the metal chest upstairs which is supposed to be a secret but which she knows all about and has opened many times with the key hidden in the china sheep. She will be glad not to have to look at it any more. The objects inside it lean with all their weight against her heart, especially the table cloth with its pattern of small green leaves, and the golden earrings which she knows belonged to the Padre's wife.

The only thing she's tempted to take with her that isn't hers, is Mr Byrd's straw hat. He never wears it, and the only time she's ever seen him with it was the day he arrived, just after she'd returned from town. She'd watched him from the window of the Padre's daughter's old bedroom, walking up the drive with it, as if he expected the weather to be hot, only to discover when he got here that it wasn't. It had hung from his hand, raindrops falling from the straw brim. Since then it's been sitting on top of the chest in his bedroom and she's sneaked in many times now to try it on (much easier since he'd followed her advice and left his windows a little ajar so the air could circulate inside). When she re-shapes the hat's brim in front of the mirror and puts it on her head, she looks like Patsy Cline.

Well, not exactly, but a little.

56

Mr Byrd, Jamshed noticed, was wearing a new style of clothing and growing a patchy sort of beard and moustache.

He was also still going to church on Sundays, and to his Tuesday evening Bible study group. He seemed full of energy. A little nervous perhaps – the twitch under the corner of his left eye had never quite gone away – but he smiled a lot and in between his long silences, was very talkative.

This morning he'd told Jamshed to drive up and down the Mysore Road and not stop anywhere, and at first he'd been quiet, but then he'd begun to speak, this time about something he'd never talked about before – something which had happened a long time ago when he was a young man in his twenties.

He was at his library, he said. Christmas was coming. Paper snowflakes were stuck on all the windows. A Christmas tree with a silver star on top stood in a bucket of sand next to the door. He was in the middle of shelving an armful of gardening books when suddenly he'd had a terrible feeling. A crashing headache, his legs so watery and weak he thought he was going to collapse.

It was the strangest thing, said Mr Byrd. He'd known something awful was about to happen. It was the only time in his life he'd ever experienced such a feeling. On his watery legs he'd gone to the telephone and dialled the number of the department store where his sister worked but she wasn't there. She'd gone out to get a cup of coffee, he was told. She would be back in five minutes. He could hold on if he liked, or he could call back. Then, out of the phone – BOOM! The biggest explosion he'd ever heard.

Jamshed glanced up into the rear-view mirror.

'Explosion, sir?'

'Yes, Jamshed. A terrible one. Paving stones and bricks and pieces of parked cars and all the nasty little pieces inside the bomb flying all over the place. It was awful. A few minutes later we saw it on the TV. Bodies everywhere. Blood. Sirens. People screaming and crying. Wyn was so lucky. Just a tiny piece of shrapnel in her left hand. It was a famous event. December 17th 1983. Part of the Troubles.'

'Troubles?'

'Yes, Jamshed. Irish people fighting British people. Catholic people fighting Protestant people. Bombs all over the place. London, Belfast, Brighton, Birmingham. You never knew when the next one was going to come.'

Mr Byrd had been quiet then. They were near the lake, and he'd sat looking out past the auto's blue tarpaulin curtain at the murky water.

'No place anywhere, sir, people not fighting,' said Jamshed.

'Yes, I suppose that's true,' said Mr Byrd, but he sounded distracted, as though he wasn't actually listening; as if he was already thinking about something else entirely, and the only reason he'd been talking just now about his past was because it seemed so far away, and because even its half-anticipated explosions – like noisy librarians and vanishing dictionaries – no longer had any power to frighten him or make him unhappy.

57

'Close your eyes.'

He loves the way she not only closes them, but also places a hand over each eye, as if she doesn't trust herself not to look.

It's one of the things he loves most about her, that she is so hungry for the world, for everything it might contain. To extend the moment, he kisses each one of her eight knuckles in turn and, with his face separated from hers only by her hands, feels her eyelashes quiver against his in the spaces between her fingers.

'You're looking!'

'I am not!'

'You are. I can feel your eyelashes moving. Now. Wait.'

Priscilla squeezes her eyes shut behind her hands. She has no idea what he is up to. She loves this about him, the way he makes a moment go on for so long it is almost unbearable. The sounds are confusing though – a rustle and a shuffle, a kicking up of leaves. Heavy – very heavy – breathing.

She screams when she sees the horse. He is so far beyond anything she expected – so outside anything she has ever imagined. 'Oh, Ravi.' She walks around the horse five times. She smooths his tail and his mane with her hand. She walks around him another five times. 'Hello, hello, hello, hello,' she says, and then, smothering his pink spongy nose with kisses, begins to tap out a lazy rhythm with her leather boot on the forest floor, and with her cheek pressed to his wide black nostrils, to sing the opening lines of *Since I Fell for You*. Then she sings the rest, and in between the words and the phrases she kisses Stephen's nose again and again, until eventually Ravi says (laughing with all his teeth showing), 'What about me?' and then it's Priscilla's turn to laugh and say, 'What about you?'

They always met at night now.

Ever since Priscilla had practically walked into Mr Byrd on her way out of the forest into the garden, it seemed safer.

In the evenings, Mr Byrd never came out of his bungalow once he'd gone into it after their lessons, and the Padre either went out on his Bun Run or sat up late at his desk in the drawing room with the door closed, working or talking to his dead wife.

As long as she was back before he went to bed, there seemed no chance he would discover she wasn't in the house. As for Ooly making any kind of fuss when she saw Priscilla walking past her sink in the dark, Priscilla thought even an earthquake was unlikely to rouse her.

The path began above the wall behind the boiler house, and from there it snaked up into the forest. A dozen steps from the kitchen door and she was on it, stumping quickly over the slippery leaf-covered ground.

Ravi took a different route – in through the presbytery's gateless opening and from there into the fringe of trees along the driveway and up round the back of the hill to their meeting place. He was always there first, waiting for her. It seemed a long time now since the beginning when they'd met only in the sheltered corner of the market stall that sold the CDs and exchanged their whispered enthusiasms – their own particular favourites and the ones it turned out they already shared. Johnny Cash and Lyle Lovett. Bonnie Raitt and Patsy Cline. With the market going on all around them, humming snatches of songs.

'Now,' said Priscilla. 'Play.'

So Ravi played. He played and he sang. All week he'd been practising *Achy Breaky Heart*, and when he finished Priscilla said it was good, but it needed to be better, and by the way in the second verse, he was still singing 'our car seats' instead of 'Arkansas' which was what was written down in the lyrics. 'OK,' said Ravi, and sang it again. He sang 'Arkansas' and not 'our car seats' and nodded his head to the yearning repetition of the chorus. He strummed and he strummed, and although she was as nervous as if a crowd of thousands sat before the two of them in the darkness, on the sixth go-through Priscilla took a deep breath and picked a pine cone from the ground and swung it up to her lips like a microphone and with what she hoped resembled the full throaty snap and bounce of Billy Ray Cyrus, she began, also, to sing.

It will not rain tonight. Both of them have looked up at the white sky today and felt the familiar shifts of the damp air in their skins and in their bones and know it will be morning before the rain comes again. The ground, though, is soft and wet, and Priscilla has taken the precaution of bringing her new felt poncho to spread beneath them. They lead Stephen a little distance away, into the trees, and while Priscilla whispers quietly to him about the future, Ravi hobbles the horse's front legs to keep him from wandering. 'There,' he says, and Priscilla takes his hand, and then Stephen is alone. He breathes in the pleasant mushroomy perfume of the forest and savours the light sprinkle of moisture falling onto his back from the canopy of leaves above. There are sounds he recognises and others he doesn't, but after a while there is singing, which is always a treat, the human voice at its best.

58

It was raining when Henry Page's letter arrived.

It had a young man's scruffiness about it: a thin, brown and in no way special envelope, the stamps with their little red maple leaves askew in the corner, the writing cramped and untidy and crowded over to the left. But it contained great and unexpected tidings and after he'd finished reading it, the Padre sat for a long time behind his desk, telling his dead wife, Vallie, in a voice full of emotion that everything, in the end, had worked out, all his prayers had been answered.

He could hardly wait to tell Priscilla. All this time, and everything – her whole future – right here under their noses.

A great weight that had been pressing down on him seemed to lift from his shoulders like a physical thing.

He would tell her this evening about the young man's proposal.

In the meantime he was bursting to tell *someone,* and he had already told the dog, who had shown no interest or excitement whatsoever. How happy he was, therefore, half-way through the afternoon, to see the familiar bouncing shape of Mr Hilary Byrd's favourite auto rattling towards the presbytery through the driveway's puddles – Mr Byrd, whose arrival here in the hills seemed, all in all, to have brought with it one good thing after another.

59

Frances Moreland began (slowly) to play and the congregation to sing, and when it was over the Padre started to speak.

Once he got going Byrd had difficulty understanding what he was saying; when he spoke quickly and with feeling, as he did when he was in the pulpit, the rhythm of his English was so strange it sounded like a different language.

Now, in his mind's eye, he replayed yesterday's encounter with the old clergyman: the way he'd come hurrying towards him, talking excitedly and incomprehensibly, with the brown envelope aloft in his hand. He had known at once, from the Padre's jubilation, that it contained terrible news.

He leafed through the Bible on the narrow shelf built into the pew in front.

Hold that fast what thou hast, he read, *that no man take thy crown.*

Ha.

Well.

And how was he supposed to do that? What crown?

He thought that he had always known things would not go smoothly. Sometimes he thought all the worst surprises of his life were things he expected to happen because they were the very things he was most afraid of. Not the IRA bomb. The IRA bomb had been different. The bomb had been extraordinary. Before the bomb, he'd experienced something physical – a premonition in the coldness of his blood of something awful he couldn't imagine. This was completely different. This was a surprise, but now that it had happened, he knew that like the deaths of his mother and his Aunt Peggy, he'd been expecting it.

Beneath the lightness and optimism of the past two weeks, it seemed to him now that there'd been a dread of something like this being thrown across his path, and here it was.

Last night he'd lain in his pyjamas, listening to the sounds of the night outside his window, thinking sometimes that between the distant trundle of cars and trucks beyond the trees and the screech of the barking deer and the much closer plock-plock that might be the rain or might be an insect, he could make out the squelch and splash of human feet coming up along the drive: Henry Page already arriving to put an end to everything before he and Priscilla had even had a chance to begin.

After church he didn't go anywhere. He didn't go trotting down the broad concrete steps to where the old man would be waiting to take him anywhere he wanted to go. He tried to tell himself it was because of the weather, which after the warmth of the last few weeks, had turned cold and wet again. He tried to tell himself he wouldn't feel so bad if it weren't for the drizzle and the chilly mountain wind, which had so delighted him when he arrived but was now so dispiriting. He did not dwell for long, though, on the weather. He lay on his bed, thinking about the young missionary.

He tried to imagine what he might look like.

He knew he must be tall, as tall as Byrd himself was. Byrd knew it from his clothes, which for the past fourteen days he'd been wearing himself. Other than that, all he knew for certain was that he was young, and that he was good.

The Padre had spoken often about the goodness of Henry Page – that as well as helping at St Peter's, he worked at the women's refuge and played basketball with the children at the orphanage and once a week took the bus out to the leper colony; that at night he went with the Padre on the Padre's Bun Run; that he went to church and to Frances Moreland's Tuesday evening Bible study group, and Byrd knew that when Henry Page did those things, he was not pretending, he was not an impostor, he was a proper Christian, and on top of everything, he was young. He was everything, in short, that Byrd wasn't, and Priscilla and the Padre would choose him, surely, a hundred times over someone like himself.

He felt in every way a fool. Henry Page. Absent but in the wings. The whole, entire time.

All night he lay awake, and when he thought matters couldn't get any worse, the following day, in the presbytery, he disturbed a pile of papers on the Padre's desk while preparing for his English lesson with Priscilla, and came upon a photograph he'd never seen before. The Padre, who saw him looking, beamed and said, 'That, sir, is Mr Henry Page.'

Ah. So he was also handsome. Of course.

Long-haired and sun-burnished and rangy and athletic. Coloured threads circled his wrists and a leather necklace hung around his neck with something silvery attached to it in the loose V of his open shirt; a cross no doubt.

Byrd's heart tightened and seemed to shrink and burrow into his chest, as if it were trying to defend itself. That old feeling he'd had when he was a boy, of being perpetually measured against some standard he couldn't possibly achieve.

He couldn't remember ever having felt as exposed, though, as he did now – so conscious of his own defects; of his age, and his bony body, his little paunch, his need of reading glasses, his thinning hair and his anxiety about money, his stupid new beard, his absence of faith, his need of butter and dried fruit and small books full of colourful illustrations to bring himself close to Priscilla.

He was still wearing the young man's clothes, the same clothes Henry Page was wearing in the photograph. He felt the Padre looking at him, and glimpsed himself in the broken silvering of the presbytery's drawing room mirror – a grotesque figure, a desperate gnome tricked out in another man's bright, borrowed garments. He made his excuses to the Padre and hurried away, pleading a headache that would make it impossible for him to teach Priscilla this evening. In his bungalow he pulled off the plaid shirt and shook off the many-pocketed trousers and sat in his underwear on his bed with his hands on his knees for a long time without moving.

He wished he was handsome like Henry Page. Handsome, and young, and good. A prince. He might have a chance against him then. As it was, he felt inferior to him in every possible way.

Slowly he gathered up the boy's crumpled discarded clothes from the floor and hung them again on the hook behind the bedroom door and dressed himself in his own things.

He remembered an evening at home last year when he'd been shopping, for the first time in his life, on the internet, for a new pair of trousers. Wyn had suggested he try it – it would be more painless, she said, than going up to London or trailing up and down Bromley High Street. If he didn't feel like going out, she'd said gently, he didn't have to. He could do everything from home. From a selection on the screen he'd picked out a pair of maroon corduroys, and with his choice, a message had appeared: People who bought these also bought *Barchester Towers* and *The Decline and Fall of the Roman Empire*. It had shocked him, to be so precisely categorised; so comprehensively measured and accurately appraised.

He thought of Wyn now, at home in England, and wondered what she was doing, if she was sleeping or pottering about in the rooms of their house in the early hours of her own faraway morning. Her letters lay in a pile on his desk. The stamps looked strange and foreign. He picked one up at random and opened it. It was from September and he read that the weather had been unseasonably warm; that Wyn had been eating her breakfast in the garden. That she'd driven down to Margate with Kathryn from work to see the big new gallery there. That she missed him. That she was very happy everything was going well, and that he was feeling so much better.

He pictured her in the garden, eating her cereal and her toast, and for the first time in many weeks, he wished she was here, because he was feeling a sort of loosening all around him, a slipping away of everything which had come to feel solid and important; a slipping through his fingers of everything he'd done and discovered by himself – of everything which in spite of the strange unfamiliarity of his surroundings, he'd thought might be enduring. He thought of the photograph on the Padre's desk of Henry Page, wearing his pom-pom hat with its dangling earflaps; his wide, winning smile. The low-slung jeans on his narrow hips, the wafer-thin object in one of his hands which looked like a small computer or an electronic book. He lay down on his bed and thought of his own enormous suitcase, full of the books he'd dragged along with him on his journey because he'd been worried about running out of things to read. Across the room on the opposite wall the stitched words of the embroidered placard mocked him. *Lean Not On Thine Own Understanding*. Well. His understanding had been clouded by hope. He had little hope now. When he thought of Henry Page, the prospect of his imminent return, he pictured the slow relentless way aeroplanes have of approaching when seen from the ground, and he was shocked by it – the violence of his hate.

60

As far as he can tell – the investigating officer will say to the superintendent of police – he has everything straight now. The precise sequence of events.

Everything, the investigating officer will say to the superintendent, was clear enough to him now – who did what when and why. As far as he could see, it was a simple enough story. So much passion simmering under the surface of things. Always, every once in a while, the lid blowing off, and nothing, it seemed, that anyone could do to stop it happening.

61

Today Mr Byrd is telling his story of Grace.

How he is tucking into his big fish when the Padre is praying and giving thanks to heaven for food.

Mr Byrd's mouth full, embarrassed.

Padre asking Christian Sir?

Mr Byrd saying Lord no!

The old man slipped the rose-coloured exercise book back in its place on the pile. It seemed a long time ago, Mr Byrd telling him about his first dinner with the Padre. The tasty food, his hasty tucking in, the Padre's question. Mr Byrd's *Lord no!* – his embarrassment.

Now Mr Byrd was going to church and attending Bible classes. For a while he had been dressed in clothes which had not looked like his own but now he was wearing his old familiar garments. It was all very confusing.

Byrd thought of confiding in the old driver, but found that he couldn't.

Instead he circled around it all, wanting and needing to talk about it, to broach the subject in some way, but without confessing his situation.

'I was hoping, I think, Jamshed,' he said eventually as they clattered past the southern entrance of the market, 'to meet someone here, but I haven't. I haven't met anyone.'

Jamshed was silent.

He eased his small vehicle into the flow of traffic, squeezing the green rubber horn.

They were heading to the racecourse, which Byrd had not yet visited.

He'd never watched a horse race except on television. He and Wyn had placed a bet once on the Grand National, the year of Red Rum, and they'd watched then, and another time he recalled when there'd been a terrible accident at Becher's Brook. Now, as they cruised closer, he could hear the thunder of hoofbeats and the rapid and excited commentary which was being broadcast across the course. It was so fast and ebullient Byrd couldn't tell if it was in English or something else. They drifted to a stop in front of a pair of tall iron gates. He leaned forward, trying to catch a glimpse of the race. 'What are they saying, Jamshed?'

'One horse winning, sir. Thirty yards.'

'Wait for me here, Jamshed,' said Byrd.

As he walked his legs felt uncertain beneath him, as if whatever scaffolding had been holding him up these last few weeks had suddenly given way. He hadn't slept since the arrival of the missionary's letter; had told himself it would be a good thing to go out today and try in some small way to distract himself, to look at something new. At the library he'd seen old photographs of the racecourse – its white, turreted buildings and beautifully kept swathe of turf.

'Oh my,' he whispered.

A ghostly ruin of stucco lay before him.

High up in the roofless pavilion he could see, like a pair of church bells, the loudspeakers which provided the raucous commentary. Beneath them, a group of men in rain jackets huddled with their betting slips. Out on the track, shawled women were planting cabbages.

'Are there ever any races here any more, Jamshed?'

'No, sir. Radio broadcast only.'

'How very disappointing.'

Byrd heard his own voice, tetchy and irritable. He couldn't help it. He wanted to blame someone for everything.

'Sorry, sir.'

In the days that followed, Byrd walked a lot, slept, brooded, occasionally ate, and buried himself in the reading room of the old library.

He read about the construction of the railway – the army of labourers and locomotive builders and engineers, materials procurers, clerks, explosives, bullocks, carpenters, painters, picks, saws, map makers, cooks, horses, tents, carts, chains, timber, steel, soldiers on horseback, soldiers in boots on the ground, in woollen uniforms, barefoot men in almost no clothes at all and men in sandals, spectators, wives in horse-drawn carriages, curious children, mountains of blasted rock and torn up trees and earth, rubble lifted out of a winding seam in the mountainside and carted away, a vein opened in the rock to lay the tracks, a toothed cable to haul the pretty blue train all the way up into the sky. Everything measured, everything recorded. Photographed. In the evenings, camp fires dotting the broken escarpment. Sixteen years of blasting and building and labour but a wonder when it was finished. No record, as far as Byrd could see, of how many perished in the course of its construction but the whole enterprise considered a triumph by the British who, before the railway, were obliged to labour up the mountainside and across rivers and up and down gorges and through thick forests on horseback, or riding bullock carts; who, before the railway, must have felt that no sooner had they arrived – no sooner had they unpacked their flannel underwear and their hot water bottles and thrown open the windows to air the pleasant rooms of their newly built houses or bungalows and taken a stroll around their garden in the delicious cool air – than it was practically time to pack up again and return to their work down in the heat of the plains. One of the Collectors, Byrd read, before the arrival of the railway, so dreaded the return that he refused to leave. He wanted to stay in the hills with his hot water bottle and his flannel underwear, his raspberry canes and his begonias. His officials wrote to him from Madras but their letters piled up unopened on a tray in the hallway.

The train, he read, had four sets of brakes.

The track was twenty-nine miles long; the journey precisely as slow now as it was a hundred years ago: five hours up, and three and a half down.

There were 208 curves, sixteen tunnels and 250 bridges.

Byrd recalled that at one point, on his own journey up, he had looked out of the window, back at the snaking blue carriages behind, and felt almost faint at the plunging view behind and below: the carriages rattling along the narrow track that teetered atop four or five thin brick columns rising up out of the trees and vegetation beneath. It was like being hauled up, out of the depths, inch by inch, on the end of a powerful mechanical finger. He remembered how refreshed he'd felt, how elated. As if he were leaving all his difficulties at the bottom of the mountain, like an unwanted bag, or his own worn-out skin.

He closed the book and returned it to the shelf where he'd found it, in the transport section. He scanned the spines of others for something to read. There were books about ships and aeroplanes and submarines. There was a book about space rockets and one about bicycles, and tucked between a volume about tractors and another about combine harvesters, there was a short pamphlet about the invention of the rickshaw.

He pulled it out and went back to his chair.

The word *rickshaw*, he read, originated from the Japanese word *jinrikisha* (人力車, 人 *jin* = human, 力 *riki* = power or force, 車 *sha* = vehicle). It was a vast improvement, said the book, in terms of the comfort and smoothness of the ride, on its precursors, the sedan chair and the palanquin, and still as cheap as either, man-power being far less expensive than horse-power.

No one, it seemed, could agree on where the first ever rickshaw was made, or by whom.

Some said it was invented in 1869 by two men in Japan, Suzuki Tokujiro, and Takayama Kosuke; others said that Tokujiro and Kosuke didn't actually dream up the machine but joined forces with a person called Izumi Yosuke, who did. Others said no, it was an American missionary in Japan, Jonathan Scobie. Scobie, they said, built the first ever rickshaw to transport his invalid wife through the streets of Yokohama.

Not so, according to another account, which placed the invention in the burly hands of an American blacksmith named Albert Tolman, at a forge in Worcester, Massachusetts, in 1846, a full 23 years before anyone in Japan had thought of such a thing. Tolman, the story went, invented the rickshaw (or what he called a 'man-drawn lorry') for a local missionary bound for South America.

Byrd looked up from the pages of the book. Through the library's tall windows he could see the silvery tops of the eucalyptus trees tossing in the wind. So many missionaries! He almost laughed. His life, suddenly, seemed to be full of them. Jonathan Scobie in Yokohoma. The other one setting out from Albert Tolman's forge for South America. Henry Page.

Henry Page, Henry Page, Henry Page.

On Sunday he went to church, and on the following Tuesday, to Frances Moreland's Bible study group.

He arrived early, and being early and seeing no one about, wandered into the garden behind the house where, on the ancient court, the men from the expensive boarding school – the headmaster and the buildings supervisor – were playing tennis.

From the steps in front of the French windows he watched them leaping about. They were both very good. The headmaster, in spite of his bulk, was extremely fast on his feet and hit the ball with such force that Byrd gasped – the ball seemed to be heading like a bullet for his opponent, but the buildings supervisor returned the shot with what seemed to Byrd like very determined ambition. He himself had never played tennis – he'd never been sporty, it was one of the aspects of school he'd found so rebarbative: the endless picking of teams and running of races. When the two men had finished and the old court was empty, he stepped away from the old square house that had once belonged to Frances Moreland's great-aunt, and went out there. He played a few imaginary strokes by himself, then over in the corner of the court he rested his arm on the handle of the big rusted roller. When it tipped forwards he lost his balance and fell over. He looked up and saw Frances at the window. She waved. She was smiling warmly at him, and it occurred to him that she was fond of him and that everything would be easy if he was fond of her too.

They read about the Flood, and afterwards at the door, Frances Moreland repeated her invitation, that he was welcome at any time to visit and look through her great-aunt's books and he said, thank you, that was a kind offer.

Out on the road Jamshed was waiting to collect him.

The rain was pouring down. Water foamed across the windscreen of the tiny vehicle like the rinse cycle in a car wash and blew in through the tarpaulin across his lap, soaking him. He paid the old man with a soft sopping note, and over the splosh and clatter of the deluge, paddled across the lawn to the concrete steps that led to his bungalow.

He broke a fistful of sticks on his knees over the hearth and built a pyramid in the grate, pushing balls of newspaper into the centre and lighting them, but the damp wood failed to take the flame and he had no more newspaper.

He brushed his teeth and changed into his pyjamas, and for an hour he tried to read, but mostly he sat in his bed, propped up against his pillow, looking around at the now familiar details of his bungalow. His eyes travelled over everything – the rug and the curtains, the embroidered exhortations on the walls in their wooden frames, the chest with its three deep drawers and the mirror above it. He saw his own face reflected there and for a long time he stared at it, as if he were searching in its bony hills and valleys for something he had not yet found. He had longed for coolness, but here in his bungalow it was damp and chilly and cheerless. It was full of hollow spaces and a creeping, penetrating cold. The blackened sticks from his failed fire lay collapsed in the hearth. Outside the rain fell.

He wished the Canadian missionary did not exist. He wished tomorrow would be another day like the ones before his letter had come.

That night he dreamed of rain. Rain pouring out of the sky in such a deluge it was like someone bleeding to death. He was out on the hill, in the dream, the water up to his waist, a tiny spoon in a furious swirling cup of dirty, tea-coloured water. Terrible things came rushing past – a bus and a fruit truck, a piano and a rowing boat and Jamshed's yellow auto. Nothing seemed alive any more, then out of the gateless entrance to the presbytery came the dog, Ooly, on the hope chest, riding the torrent and reaching out to him and calling, 'Uncle!' and then the hope chest was upon him, looming and large like a Cross Channel ferry, pushing him under, ploughing over his head, speeding along on top of the water and down along the drowned railway to Mettupalayam and the plains and far, far away.

62

'We will miss you, Mr Byrd, when you leave.

'Falling over, locking out – our lives are full of excitement since you came to us. Every day is different. I thank God for sending you! We make scones and meringues and shortbread and new clothes. We walk in the garden. We read. We write. We talk. And now we are to have a wedding.' The Padre nodded. 'Yes, Mr Byrd, we shall miss you, but it is as Luke says, perhaps, that we must all of us part with what is dearest to us on earth.'

Is it? Byrd wanted to say. He was tearful again, and angry. Why must we always be parted from what is dearest to us? Why is it a condition of life that we are made to love things if we are only to lose them?

'Leaving?'

The quiet surprise in Priscilla's voice sounded so much like concern that just for a moment Byrd paused.

'Priscilla, Mr Byrd is leaving us,' the Padre had said, a moment before, and because the hope of lovers is the most unreasonable thing in the universe – because it clutches at words and parses every last pause and silence and tone of voice – when Priscilla spoke, Byrd wavered.

They stood, the three of them, and for a moment it seemed possible to him that the Padre, and perhaps Priscilla too, understood his feelings. They were in the kitchen, making one last tray of shortbread, and briefly, even though everything was agreed and decided and tomorrow evening Henry Page would return, he wondered if perhaps there was another way. But neither she nor the Padre said anything to alter things – neither of them begged him not to leave – and when the Padre said it was a shame he would not have the chance to meet Mr Page, Byrd said he should probably go now, and get on with his packing.

In the Carter's Nest For Rest, before an unlit fire, he sat listening to the sounds of the evening beyond his window. He imagined being here and hearing the sound of Henry Page approaching. He imagined the young missionary coming sooner than he'd promised and finding him still here, occupying his bungalow like a cuckoo. Well, he had no wish to be here for that. He did not want to have to see the boy. He wanted now only to slip away on the old train the way he'd come. He would leave them to get on with their lives. It was like being at the library at home again. Everything had moved on without him. It was a story he had tried to write himself into but it was false. He had tried to take up the different threads in his fingers and plait them according to his wishes and that had been foolish. Only in fairy tales were there sets of tasks or barriers that were eventually accomplished or overcome; only in fairy tales were there spells that were cast and then lifted.

In the light from the presbytery that shone against the misted window between his open curtains, the book by Andersen stood on the sill above his desk. He reached up and lifted it down. On the back was a photograph of the great story-teller, long-faced and frock-coated, leaning on a chair. Something of a bore, Byrd recalled reading somewhere, who when he visited people, often stayed longer than he was welcome. People disliked him for it, for not knowing when he wasn't wanted.

Byrd made himself some supper and put his porridge to soak for the morning. Tomorrow he would say his goodbyes to the Padre and Priscilla and go into town, and on his way to the railway station he would buy some souvenirs to take home to Wyn. At the bottom of the steps below the hill outside the presbytery he would climb into the old man's auto and ask him to drive him, and when he'd finished his shopping he would catch his train. A car was booked to collect him at Mettupalayam, at the foot of the mountain, and drive him the remaining four hours to the airport. By tomorrow night, he would be home.

In the big pink bucket he washed himself and put on his pyjamas.

He spent ten minutes looking for his glasses and found them, eventually, on the edge of the sink in the bathroom. From the windowsill above his bed he took down the last of the books he'd brought in his suitcase and had yet to finish – the memoirs by Stendhal, Flaubert and Gide. He flipped through them and from one to another, unable to settle, unable to decide which life to choose. His eyes skimmed over paragraphs and pages.

My best sentences, he read, *are the ones I begin without knowing how they will end.*

63

There was a new urgency, now, to everything; Priscilla anxious that they go before the return of the Canadian missionary.

Priscilla told Ravi that the Padre talked excitedly almost all the time now about Henry Page and her future, and that more than once she's opened her mouth to speak but she can't. She can't listen to him and look at him and tell him, and anyway they are ready now with everything. Every evening for the last five days, when Ravi's finished at the salon, and before Priscilla goes with her books or her sewing to the drawing room for her lesson with Mr Hilary Byrd, they've been meeting in the forest above the presbytery to practise. Over and over. *There He Goes* and *Achy Breaky Heart* and *Stop the World and Let Me Off* and *Crazy*. It seemed to both of them they were getting better all the time. The songs sounded good and the costumes were ready.

One last time now, they would meet in the forest, and then they'd be off.

But then the horse, Stephen, fell ill.

Perhaps it was a microbe, something lingering from when he spent his days wandering across the forecourt of the Bharat Petroleum Station and along the main road, grazing from the gutters and in the big dumpster near the lakeshore. Perhaps he was older than his previous owner had claimed; perhaps he did not have as much life left in him as Ravi had been led to believe when he begged his uncle for the money to buy him.

'Are you sick?' he whispered, lying down next to the animal. He had never seen it lie down before.

'Are you an old man?'

Ravi pushed gently at Stephen's upper lip. It was spongier than usual, and whiter. It revealed long yellow teeth, and the young barber remembered hearing somewhere that you could tell the age of a horse by its teeth. If you could, he didn't know how, and lying here now, listening to the animal's laboured breaths, the high whistling that came shrilling from the black nostrils which struck him as unusually dry, Ravi felt he didn't want to know. What would he tell Priscilla? How would he break it to her that the unpromising animal he'd persuaded his uncle to buy had let them down? That he, Ravi, had literally backed the wrong horse?

Overhead the rain clattered on the tin awning attached to the back wall of the salon.

The whites of Stephen's eyes were cloudy and dark. His eyelids fluttered and closed. Ravi smoothed the thin grey hair across the animal's forehead. He laid his ear against Stephen's heaving chest, where he thought Stephen's heart might be. He could hear a kind of sloshing sound, rhythmic and low but he didn't know what it meant; he knew nothing about horses, healthy or sick, he had no idea if this was the sound of a horse in the last moments of its life. Still lying down, he stroked the suffering animal's palpitating neck. He blew softly into one of the tall pointy ears and hoped it would twitch but it didn't.

'Come on, boy,' he whispered. 'Giddyap. Please.'

64

The news travelled fast.

Like a swiftly moving wind it travelled through the congregation of St Peter's, the news that the young Canadian missionary, Henry Page, was on his way back to marry the Padre's crippled orphan housekeeper, and from the congregation of St Peter's it hurried down the hill to the expensive boarding school and the Women Workers' Co-operative, to the orphanage and even as far out as the leper colony – all through the town and beyond it, passed on from shop to shop and market stall to market stall, from house to house and person to person.

'He will be back tonight,' says one of the men, the oldest of them, who over time has become their leader.

They have gathered down by the railway tracks around a small, open bonfire. The youngest one is moving about nervously from foot to foot. Although he participated in the attack on the taxi driver in town a few weeks back, he has done nothing like this before. His wife is worried about it all and has tried to persuade him not to do it, whispering so the children won't hear them arguing, but, nervous as he is, he is not to be talked out of it. It is all too important for that.

Only he would rather it be the Padre instead of the Canadian missionary. Or the pastor at the new Believers Church out at the edge of town beyond the racecourse which was small but was growing fast; every week there seemed to be more people in there. But the others are clear that it should be the tall foreigner attached to St Peter's. St Peter's was bigger and more famous and with a foreigner it will have more impact. It will be more talked about, splashed across more newspapers and on TV and all over the internet. Also there is a general feeling among them that it has always been foreigners who are mostly to blame, more than men like the old Padre – that if it hadn't been for the foreign missionaries, the Christians would never have got anywhere; that over the centuries it is mostly the coming of the British and the Germans and the Portuguese, the Italians and the French – of the Catholics and the Protestants from abroad with their churches and their schools and their orphanages and their do-gooding – who are mostly to blame with their hundreds of years of forcing the story of Jesus Christ down people's throats, displacing the rightful gods. They had always been sneakier than the Muslims. Islam had always favoured the sword but the Christians, with their offers of education and food and shelter, had always been sneaky.

'Tonight then,' says another of the men, and another and another, until even the young one finds himself saying, 'Yes, tonight.'

65

Jamshed drifted to a stop outside the Botanical Gardens and climbed out of his auto. 'Leaving?'

The word had dropped like a stone into his heart. Mr Byrd, leaving?

For three days, Mr Byrd had not come in the mornings to their meeting place at the bottom of the concrete steps and Jamshed hadn't known what to do with himself. He picked up an Italian couple who were going to the Savoy for lunch, and a trio of Japanese tourists who wanted to go to the lake, but it wasn't the same, and after the first morning without Mr Byrd, he'd stopped looking for anyone else to drive.

It was years since he'd walked in the Gardens. He hadn't been in them since he was a young man. They had come for a picnic when Ravi was born – his father and Bipin and Deesha and Deesha's sister and a handful of times he'd come with Prem, but for most of his life he'd waited outside their big gates while others strolled along their paths and looked at the trees and shrubs and inspected the little metal markers which explained their origins and their particular qualities. On his right as he entered stood the Toda museum. He remembered visiting it on the day of the picnic and afterwards with Prem, all the artefacts inside which gave an account of the lives and customs of the people who were here before the British came and built the town.

On his left, vast, fern-filled glasshouses gleamed like sheets of water under the white sky. He walked past silver oaks and Australian conifers and beds of orange and scarlet begonias. The path climbed gradually, and at the top of the rise he sat down on an iron bench and looked out through the trees across the town below.

He missed Mr Byrd's introspective chatter, his pieces of unexpected information, his occasional questions, his stories of Petts Wood and his sister Wyn and his Aunt Peggy, his tribulations at the library, his stories about his doctor and the terrorist bomb and the lost language which had once been spoken on the little islands off the coast of Scotland. He missed his tall body folded up in the back, leaning against the rail, his anxious, curious gaze turned upon the town's buildings and trees and the contents of his shopping bag when he came out of the market.

And now yesterday he'd come again at last, only to say he was leaving. At three o'clock this afternoon he would take the train back down the mountain the way he'd come and disappear forever.

They spent the first hour of the morning calling in at different places in the town, at the market and the wholesaler and the King Star Chocolate Shop. Mr Byrd's small packages accumulated on the leatherette seat in the back of the auto, souvenirs for his sister. Some soap nuts and a packet of chocolate tea, a brown and red blanket.

'I think that's it, Jamshed. Everything I want.' Hilary Byrd looking distant and tired.

Last stop, the CTR Salon for a trim.

Outside, Ravi, with the horse, because yesterday, when

Ravi woke up on the floor of the lean-to behind the salon, Stephen's eyes were open, his black nostrils glowing with a damp, healthy sheen. He'd whinnied once and scrambled to his feet. He'd tossed back his straggly mane and swished his thin tail. His tall ears twitched. When Ravi gave him a banana, he chomped down on it hungrily. He looked better, he looked fine. He looked ready to rock and roll.

Ravi held the horse's bridle. He was dressed in his gleaming white Stetson and piebald chaps.

'Ravi leaving also,' said Jamshed sadly to Hilary Byrd, but Hilary Byrd did not reply, he was too preoccupied with his own affairs.

Inside the salon, from the barber's chair, he looked at his own face in the mirror and then all around – at the orange thermos flask of hot water and the combs and scissors in their jar of bright blue liquid, the motionless ceiling fan with its dangling beaded cord. With Ravi outside with the horse and ready for his journey, one of the older barbers saw to the trimming of Byrd's hair and the removal of his unsuccessful beard and the moustache which went with it and seemed now, to Byrd, as ridiculous as a stray caterpillar.

At the Assembly Rooms he sat in the dark on one of the velvet-upholstered seats. It was still not yet the middle of the morning and there was no one else. He was quite alone. The film was a Western, full of horses and men in large hats and ponchos, but Byrd was distracted and paid no attention.

After that he sat in the back of the old driver's auto munching chocolate and not talking.

'Piece of chocolate, Jamshed?' he offered, eventually, leaning forward with the open silver bag between his fingers.

The old man shook his head. Thank you, but no. He wasn't hungry today.

It was a mad, aberrant thing the old driver did.

After the Assembly Rooms he told Hilary Byrd he needed to go to his hut to fetch some money to give to his nephew for his journey. Would Sir mind stopping there with him? He could wait in his hut while Jamshed went back to the salon to give his nephew the money. 'I will be very quick, sir. One half hour only.'

The old man's heart was beating very fast. He had never lied to Hilary Byrd before and had no plan beyond making sure he missed his train; no plan beyond padlocking the door of his hut with Hilary Byrd inside and not returning for two hours. He could see it was senseless, that there would be another train tomorrow, and another the day after, and every day after that – endless opportunities for Mr Hilary Byrd to leave and go home and never come back.

'So this is yours, Jamshed?' said Byrd, peering around the hut's interior.

The old driver gave a kind of bow. 'Yes, sir.'

He had not wanted to bring Mr Byrd to his home but it was all he could think of.

Byrd saw walls made of the flattened panels of bright blue Kingfisher drums, a corrugated roof; a narrow bed with a red cotton coverlet, a box with a green cloth over it, a cooking ring on top of a blue 30 kilogram gas canister like the one in his bungalow, a rug on the floor. An exercise book with a curling rose-coloured cover, on top of it a blue biro with half the ink used up.

The old man pushed the book into the box with the green cloth over it and reached under the bed and drew out a jar of folded notes.

'For nephew.'

If Sir would wait, he would be back in half an hour.

Hilary Byrd nodded. He was tired, drained of life and energy. 'You go, Jamshed. I'll sit here till you come back.'

The old man ducked out of the door, which was made of wood and hung in an opening cut in one of the tin panels and secured it with the thick bolt of the J. J. Legge padlock.

It was a stupid thing to do, he knew it was, to lock the door, and when he returned, two and a half hours later, after the scheduled departure of Hilary Byrd's train, Hilary Byrd shouted at him, and perhaps it was because Byrd was thinking bitterly of all the foolish hours he'd spent in church and at Frances Moreland's Bible study group that when he shouted at the old man his words came out in a bitter and furious kind of Commandment: 'THOU SHALT NOT, JAMSHED, LOCK THY CUSTOMER IN THY TIN SHACK!'

The old man looked down at his broken, mismatched footwear. *Thy customer.* It was almost as if they had returned to their very first day together, when Hilary Byrd had ignored him and pushed past him and dragged the wheels of his suitcase over his toes.

'Sorry, sir,' he said humbly. It was a mistake, he said. It was his habit always to lock his hut when he left it.

All the way back to the presbytery they rode in silence. At the bottom of the bungalow steps the old man dropped Hilary Byrd off with his packages and Byrd did not ask him to return in the morning to take him to the railway station. It broke his heart, all of it. Half of him wishing Mr Byrd would not leave, half of him wishing that he had never come.

66

Doubt.

It arrived without warning, at Schiphol airport, with the girl who'd been across the aisle from him on the flight from Montreal. At Schiphol they sat in a cafe waiting for their connections. Over coffee and a cold can of Sprite, they'd lingered until her flight came up on the board and she had to go. At the last minute, a clumsy hug and a kind of half-kiss.

'Bye then.'

'Bye.'

She was pretty and had made him laugh and when she was gone he sat thinking about her for a long time and suddenly he was not so sure any more about everything.

Or perhaps his doubts would have arrived anyway, with or without the girl.

Perhaps, being so far away, it had not seemed quite real, what he'd made up his mind to do, and the closer he got the more real it seemed and not a thing he could actually do.

In Winnipeg, it had felt like an important and necessary thing; an essential act of charity and Christian kindness. To marry Priscilla and bring her home to Canada, to fix her slightly protuberant teeth and get her a better boot for her short right leg and maybe some prosthetic thumbs and generally improve her life. In Winnipeg, he'd felt that he could not in good conscience sit down again with the Padre and watch the old man munching disconsolately on his evening bowl of fryums, listening to her clumping about in the kitchen, and the Padre's whispered tales of woe about his fruitless search, without putting himself forward. In Winnipeg, it had felt like the thing he was meant to do.

He hadn't told his mother. His mother would have been horrified. His mother didn't even want him to go back to India. She was afraid something awful would happen to him if he did – that he'd lose his passport or his inhaler or get sick and end up in some filthy government hospital. She was afraid he'd be robbed or swindled or taken advantage of in some way by the very people he was trying to help, and he knew she would see his decision to marry Priscilla in just this light. But to him, at home in Winnipeg it felt like he'd been placed by God in this very particular situation for a reason; it had felt like the good, the right thing to do, and he'd believed that he was supposed to embrace it.

Only now, he thought, perhaps he didn't want to. He wasn't convinced, as he'd been in Winnipeg, how absolutely necessary it was.

Now, as he stood looking at his new visa beneath its shiny plastic covering inside his gold and blue passport, he thought that he had bitten off more than he could chew. He was, after all, not so much a missionary as a volunteer, not so different from the other eager do-gooders who came up into the Indian hills, who ranged in age from their late teens to their early seventies or in the case of one German woman from Stuttgart who came for two months every summer to the Women Workers' Co-op, ninety-one.

Could he excuse himself? Could he do that? Would the

Padre have already told Priscilla? Would they, with relief and elation, have been celebrating and making plans? Could he explain to them that he'd got carried away? Could he find the words to say that he'd changed his mind?

He should phone the Padre. He knows he should do that; he is expected and they will be waiting for him. But it is too awful, the thought of telling them, and instead of making a phone call, he turns away from the gate and heads over to the Air Canada desk, to see when the next flight leaves and if it will be possible to change his ticket. Back home in Winnipeg he'll take some time to think, to make new plans and find another suffering, poverty-stricken place where he can do his good works. Somewhere a little closer to home, perhaps. Maybe Bolivia. His mother will be happy.

67

Of course, said the Padre. It was no bother at all for Mr Byrd to stay one more night in the bungalow. He would accommodate Mr Page, when he arrived later this evening, in the presbytery, in his daughter's old bedroom.

'Thank you,' said Byrd. He would be off in the morning to catch his train. He had arranged for a taxi to come and collect him.

There was a brief awkwardness between them. Having already said their goodbyes once, it seemed silly to be saying them all over again, but they shook hands, and the Padre said, 'Safe travels, Mr Byrd, and God bless you.'

In his bungalow Byrd tried to remember what it had been like to be unbearably hot. This morning when he'd set off for what he thought was the last time, he'd worn warm clothes so he wouldn't be cold for the first half of his journey, hoping that the car collecting him from Mettupalayam would have air conditioning. But perhaps he'd be better off tomorrow braving the morning chill in a pair of shorts, and being freezing cold for the first half of his train journey, rather than risk being horribly uncomfortable for the second half. Or should he start off, as he'd done today, by wrapping up, and then try and change on the train into some lighter things? He didn't know, he couldn't decide. Even now, he didn't want to believe that he was leaving.

He stepped out into the garden.

In the presbytery there was no sign of life. Priscilla must have gone to bed, the Padre into town to distribute his buns, and Ooly was nowhere to be seen. She was neither in her sink nor sitting at his feet looking up at him beseechingly, and for the first time he wished she was. Even with the old driver, Jamshed, who for so long had been his almost constant companion, everything had ended badly. His solitude crashed over him and aloud in the gloaming he said, 'I have been forsaken.'

He ran his fingers over the star-shaped flowers of the sweet william, touched the heads of the hydrangea with the palm of his hand. At the Global Internet Cafe he'd sent an email to Wyn with his flight number and arrival time. Would she risk the traffic and collect him in the car? he wondered, walking slowly along the edge of the lawn and pausing in front of the huge plastic-looking shrub whose name he had never learned. Or would she come by train? Either way, he could hardly imagine it. Even after all his goodbyes, he could not picture himself so far away.

In his bungalow he struck a match and adjusted the flame beneath the Ideal Pigeon stove to boil water for his rice. He chopped an onion and a clove of garlic, and tore open a packet of biryani paste.

This much the superintendent of police knew from the spent match that was there, along with the remnants of his dinner preparation, in the kitchen bin. By the looks of it, he'd also lit a fire in the sitting room, though this was no longer burning when his officers entered the bungalow in the morning with the Padre.

The Englishman's packed suitcase was next to the door, only his washbag was left out in the bathroom, a pair of long trousers and a flannel shirt laid out for his journey. The place had been swept clean, the kitchen shelves covered with fresh newspaper, the towels washed and pegged optimistically on the wire washing line.

68

He couldn't sleep.

Sometime around one o'clock he thought he saw, through his bedroom window, a movement in the trees, in the darkness beyond the border of the garden. He remembered the day Priscilla had emerged suddenly and without warning from the forest and almost bumped into him. One moment he'd been alone among the snapdragons and the rhubarb, the penstemons and the elderflower, the next moment, there she was. *Uncle*, she'd called him, and for the first time, it had hurt his heart.

He swung his legs over the edge of his bed and fetched the torch the Padre had given him when he first arrived. *Always carry a flashlight, sir! We do not want you falling into a drain. If you fall into a drain you could drown!*

What was he thinking tonight? That it might be Priscilla emerging again from the forest, coming to him to say, Please don't go?

The rain, from the threshold of his open front door, looked like snow, spiralling in the wobbly yellow beam, and briefly Byrd thought he saw another movement, a kind of black ripple like a length of flung silk that was darker than the darkness of the trees, but whether it was an animal or a person, he couldn't tell. If it was the famous leopard the Padre's wife claimed to have glimpsed, he couldn't see it. The silhouettes of the shrubs and flowers in the borders looked the same as they always did; the only thing that was different was the dog, who wasn't in her sink. After a few minutes' peering into the night, he turned off the torch and went back inside, climbed into his bed and tried, again, to sleep.

69

Child's play, of course, to come in through the gateless opening of the presbytery garden past the useless plastic sign and enter the missionary's bungalow, the windows open a crack, a cool fresh breeze blowing in on the night's dark velvet.

When the first small creaking sounds came, Byrd thought it might be the dog, Ooly, pleading with him, in her old way, to be allowed to join him.

He could see that there were five of them; five thin figures with weapons of various shapes and sizes, dropping like cats from the windows of the verandah room and coming quietly to surround him. They pulled him off the bed and onto his knees, speaking quickly in low voices to each other in their own language. He put up his hands to defend himself but they took hold of his hair and forced his head back so he was looking up at them, into their faces and into their eyes. 'No,' Byrd heard himself say, and tried to scuttle away from them. He heard one of them give what sounded like a short, sharp command, and then they were still.

Perhaps they had a sense of theatre, or wanted to give a ceremonial air to what they were doing, or perhaps they were confused – surprised to find an oldish man when they'd been expecting a youngish one.

Anyway, they paused, and there was silence.

Byrd crouched on the floor. He tried to move but he couldn't.

High up in his throat his heart pounded and he couldn't speak. Then one of them – the one who'd never done anything like this before and was trembling with nerves and passion – spoke, in English, to Hilary Byrd.

Was he, he asked, in a not quite steady voice, the Canadian missionary, Henry Page?

And just for a moment, while the men stood and did not act, Byrd remembered the Padre's stories. Over dinner in the dim light of the presbytery he had hardly listened to them. How distant they had seemed to him, how far away from the struggles of his life. But they came back to him now, and in the lightly moving air of the little bungalow the young man's question hung so close to his face he seemed to feel its breath against his cheek.

From somewhere beyond the garden he heard the cry of the barking deer, the shuffle of the trees. Fleetingly, he heard the familiar plock-plock sound which might be the rain or might be an insect, and just for a moment he imagined himself elsewhere. Just for a moment he saw himself climbing into his taxi – his suitcase and his bundle of souvenirs on the seat next to him, his hat on top of his suitcase, his train ticket in his hand. He saw himself in the garden with Wyn and walking in the grounds of Eltham Palace. He saw himself standing in the kitchen stirring eggs and butter into a bowl of flour, and getting out his Aunt Peggy's Bernina to make new curtains for his bedroom. He saw himself taking the bus to the library to see Margaret, and finishing off any remaining paperwork connected with his leaving. Because just for a moment it seemed to Hilary Byrd that in spite of his terrible disappointment, his time here in the hills had done him good.

Just for a moment, while the men paused, he was aware that he was better, now, than when he'd arrived. He had been a teacher for a while, and for seventeen and a half weeks, he had fended entirely for himself, without Wyn. He had shopped for himself and cooked for himself. He had got up out of bed almost every day. He'd gone exploring. He had learned how to use a treadle sewing machine and discovered many other interesting new things and although there was still a lot he didn't know, he knew more now than he had when he'd come. He didn't imagine there would be a place for him in any library at home, but perhaps there were other things he could try, and just for a moment he saw himself saying all this to Wyn; telling her about his travels, his ups and his downs while he'd been away, and talking to her about his future.

But mostly it was Henry Page he saw – Henry Page who he saw more clearly, even, than he could see himself. Henry Page on an aeroplane, and in a taxi, and on the slow blue train. Henry Page splashing along the puddled driveway to the presbytery and bounding up the concrete steps past the boiler house and Ooly's sink and stepping in through the mission house door. Henry Page with his coloured bracelets and his rucksack and his brand-new visa making his eager, good-hearted journey all the way from Winnipeg to marry Priscilla.

In the silence one of the men had lowered his weapon, and just for a moment Byrd saw that the others were ready to do the same; that they believed they had the wrong man, and would keep him here now and wait for the young Canadian to come.

All around and above him he could see their faces, their eyes and the lines on their fingers and the stretched skin of their knuckles, their sticks and their mattocks and their iron rods, and just for a moment he hesitated, because he longed to see where his life might go from here; what else he might still be able to do.

Above him hung the embroidered placard. *I will be your Shield, your High Tower, the Horn of your Salvation.* In his head he heard the old man's words. *We have ourselves only.* His body shook. He was so afraid. He opened his mouth. He tried to speak but he couldn't. His head was pulled too far back.

He tried again.

Yes, he said, he was the missionary, Henry Page.

70

It was raining when the old man came.

He had brought butterscotch chocolate, a small pot of neem oil.

Gifts for Mr Byrd before he went home, to say he was sorry for locking him in his shack and causing him to miss his train. Gifts so the end of everything would not feel so permanent and complete. Gifts he would leave outside the mission house door so Mr Byrd would find them when he left in the morning by whatever mode of alternative transport he'd arranged to take himself and his luggage to the railway station.

He left his auto at the gateless entrance and walked in along the earth driveway. The presbytery was dark and so were the trees but in the early twilight the words WORLD CLASS on the back of his shirt shone.

At the top of the concrete steps he stooped, and set down his two small parcels, and saw that the bungalow door was blowing open in a way that seemed strange and wrong.

He crossed the threshold and trod carefully with a beating heart, aware as he moved further inside, of the way the sticky floor was adhering to the bottom of his flip flop and his clog. He could see the outline of the enormous chair, lumpy and black in front of the fireplace, like a terrible throne. In the stone grate a fire glowed weakly, illuminating the etching of the Scottish loch above the mantlepiece. In the corner of the room, the green fridge hummed.

Mr Byrd's eyes were closed and his face, when Jamshed touched it, was very cold, and sticky like the floor. His pyjamas were wet and heavy.

'No,' said the old driver, and then again, 'No.'

First he knelt, and then he lay down next to Hilary Byrd and stroked his matted hair with his palm. He told him about the butterscotch chocolate and the neem oil, and that he had left them just outside the door and would go and fetch them in a moment. He said it had been raining when he'd walked in along the drive but he was fairly sure it would be stopping soon. He told him about his visit to the Botanical Gardens, about the ferns and the silver oaks he had seen, and the bright beds of begonias. He said it would be morning soon. He touched his cheek, his forehead and his eyelids. He wished he would speak. He did not think he could bear his sorrow if he did not hear Hilary Byrd speak again.

Byrd felt the old man's warmth, his nearness.

He remembered they'd had an argument about something, and that they'd been separated for a while, but he understood that Jamshed was with him again now. He reached for his hand.

'Stay,' he whispered.

Jamshed held him close, and Byrd seemed calm, almost peaceful. More peaceful, perhaps, than Jamshed had ever

known him to be. On the bungalow roof the rain eased and it
was quiet. All around them the house was still.

'Train is coming,' said Jamshed softly. 'Yes – look, coming
now. Five minutes only.'

71

And down on the plains, everything warmer.

Hot.

Sweat prickling beneath Priscilla's kurti under her waistcoat and the heavy poncho. Ravi taking off his Stetson and fanning his face with it. Both of them excited and afraid. When they turned, they could no longer see the mountains behind them.

Ravi reached round and held one of Priscilla's hands in his. *Crazy,* they sang quietly in their own amateur harmony. They knew that they had themselves and nothing else, and that what they needed now was for their second-hand horse to put one hoof in front of the other.

Every hour or so they ate a little of Hilary Byrd's shortbread which Priscilla had brought along in a tin, and sometimes they stopped so that Stephen could rest and have some too.

Towards evening, Priscilla dozed against Ravi's back, and because she could sense in the stringy muscles along his spine how keyed-up he was, she roused herself and sat up tall with her chin on his shoulder and whispered, *Singing boy pick up that fiddle and play that steel guitar,* which made him laugh. She felt his muscles soften and relax, and in the gloaming she thought there'd never been anything sweeter in her life than this steady forward-moving passage of theirs; the horse, Stephen, carrying them along to the easy beat of his own sway-backed stroll as if he already knew the way. Along the roadside the trees and rocks gave way to scattered tents and then to petrol stations and fruit stalls and shops. All around them the traffic dodged and weaved, and in the distance tall buildings rose into the sky and glittered like palaces.

Acknowledgements

The Mission House is a work of fiction inspired by real events in the years leading up to the rise to power of Narendra Modi's Hindu nationalist Bharatiya Janata Party (BJP) in India. In the town where Hilary Byrd seeks refuge, I have invented certain places and changed some topographical details, but anyone who knows the former British hill station of Ootacamund ('Ooty'), in the Nilgiri Hills of Tamil Nadu in south India, will recognise it in these pages.

My very grateful thanks to all who, in so many different ways, helped me to write and publish it.

Thank you to Sunita, Andrew, Jenny and Mohan for their kindness and friendship, and to Krittika Bhattacharjee for her careful reading of an early version of the manuscript.

Thank you, as ever, and always, to Michael.

Thank you to Marion Duvert, Lamorna Elmer, Sarah Goldberg, Nan Graham, Christine Lo, Anna Webber, and everyone at Granta, Scribner, The Clegg Agency and United Agents who worked on the book.

Above all, my heartfelt thanks to Bill Clegg and Bella Lacey, whose wisdom, advice, patience, and encouragement were indispensable.

WEST

WINNER OF THE WALES BOOK OF THE YEAR FICTION AWARD

RUNNER-UP FOR THE SOCIETY OF AUTHORS' MCKITTERICK PRIZE

SHORTLISTED FOR THE RATHBONES FOLIO PRIZE

'Nothing quite prepares you for the excellence of Davies' first novel,
West . . . One of the best books I've read this year . . . Miraculous'
Andrew Holgate, *Sunday Times*

Cy Bellman, American settler and widowed father, hears news which fills
him with wonder: in the deep swamps of Kentucky, huge ancient bones
have been discovered. Leaving his young daughter Bess to fend for herself,
Cy sets off to see if there is truth in the rumours that giant monsters are
living still, roaming the uncharted territory beyond the Mississippi River.

'Davies has the astonishing ability to capture a life – however
idiosyncratic – in the briefest of brushstrokes . . . Skilfully and sparely
told . . . I gobbled up *West* in a few hours, then went straight back to the
beginning and started it again' *Evening Standard*

'Not a word is wasted; the canvas is as wide as [Davies's] brush is fine . . .
You won't be able to turn back' *Guardian*

'This exquisite novel may be only 150 pages long, but boy, does it
pack a punch' *Metro*

'A real page-turner. A magnificent achievement' *Scotsman*

'*West* can be read in a sitting, but has the scope and resonance of an epic.
Not a word is wasted [and] the result is a page-turner that can stop you
in your tracks to linger over a sentence' *Daily Mail*